P9-CQJ-149

She had never experienced a moment of such sensory perfection.

The pulsing surge of the waterfall crashing behind them, the caressing embrace of the cool water touching every inch of her skin, the earthy smell of the jungle surrounding the pool, the eggshell-blue of the sky, the vivid green trees...all her senses were on overload.

But not a single one of those things was as potent—as addicting—as the man who stepped closer and swept her into his arms.

His wet, hard body met hers, and his powerful hands lifted her at the waist. Their mouths came together in a hot, carnal kiss. His warm tongue tangled and mated with hers, thrusting deeply, his hunger consuming.

The water buoyed her, and she easily wrapped her legs around his hips. Nate glided his hands down her body, caressing her stomach, her waist, her hips, her ass. Every touch was accompanied by a swish of the water, and the eroticism of it was like nothing she had ever experienced. She couldn't even imagine how good it was going to feel when he thrust into her...

New York Times bestselling author **Leslie Kelly** has written dozens of books and novellas for Harlequin Blaze and HQN Books. Known for her sparkling dialogue, fun characters and steamy sensuality, she has been honored with numerous awards, including a National Readers' Choice Award, a Colorado Award of Excellence, a Golden Quill and an *RT Book Reviews* Career Achievement Award in Series Romance. Leslie has also been nominated four times for the highest award in romance fiction, the RWA RITA® Award. Leslie lives in New Mexico with her own romantic hero, Bruce, and their daughters. Visit her online at lesliekelly.com or at her blog, plotmonkeys.com.

Shana Gray's passion is to enjoy life. She loves to travel and see the world, be with family, friends and experience the beauty that surrounds us. Many of her experiences find their way into her books. First published in 2010 as Cristal Ryder, Shana has written contemporary erotic romances for Sybarite Seductions, Lyrical Press (now Kensington) and Ellora's Cave. Her stories range from scorching quickie length to longer erotic romance novellas. Visit her online at shanagray.com or at Twitter.com/ShanaGray_1.

CONTENTS

Dear Reader,

When I was asked to write a story for a December Blaze collection, I was picturing snowflakes, jingling bells and Santa. What fun, therefore, to get to write a super-sizzling story set in a steamy island paradise! Who doesn't dream about escaping the winter blues with a decadent fun-in-the-sun vacation? Throw in a private yacht and a destination cruise, and it sounds like the dream getaway.

Unless, of course, you're the maid of honor and the bride is your recently widowed mom. Oh, and if the best man is your ex-lover who obviously didn't care much about you because he dropped off the face of the earth a year ago.

Nathan and Heather's story was such fun to write. I loved the fantasy aspect of a typical girl getting involved with a star athlete, not to mention the wedding cruise in the Caribbean. Aren't you picturing lying on a warm, sunny beach somewhere?

I hope you enjoy *Addicted to You*—and that your winter might bring a few warm, unexpected surprises.

Best wishes,

Leslie Kelly

ADDICTED TO YOU

Leslie Kelly

To my editor, Adrienne Macintosh.
Thank you for your enthusiastic support!

1

BEFORE THIS WEEK, Heather Hughes had considered multiple orgasms to be a fantasy that very few people believed in, much less experienced. Like the tooth fairy, or love at first sight, or fat-free salad dressing that actually tasted good.

She'd been wrong. Oh, so wrong.

"I think I'm going to need a defibrillator," she managed to mutter between harsh breaths. She collapsed onto a silky pile of sheets and pillows, her heart pounding wildly in her chest. Every bone in her body seemed to have melted away, along with all her strength. The wild sex-against-the-wall had been both incredibly pleasurable and aerobically challenging. The only things she could move now were her lips, which curled up into a well-satisfied smile. "Will you resuscitate me?"

"How about I do mouth-to-mouth?" Nathan asked, falling beside her, his hand finding hers in the rumpled sheets.

"I'm pretty sure you already have. A lot."

"Are you complaining?" he asked with a confident, masculine chuckle, already knowing the answer.

"Most definitely not."

God, no. Nate Watson was hands-down the best kisser she'd ever met. Best lover, too. Best looking. Smartest. Sexiest. Funniest. He was, without a doubt, the perfect man.

Hard to believe she'd only known him for seventy-two hours.

When she'd set out for a long girls' weekend get-away in Vegas, she'd never dreamed she'd meet someone so amazing. She'd certainly never expected him to ask her to extend her trip so they could spend more time together.

She'd refused at first, having responsibilities at home. She ran a shop right on the plaza in Santa Fe and seldom took vacation. But her two best friends had cheered her on, urging her to go for it, saying every woman should grab at least one wild adventure with a guy most only dreamed of meeting. She knew they were right. So once they'd promised not to tell anyone she was staying longer so she could get her freak on with a stranger she'd met at the craps tables, she'd said yes.

Heather had never done anything so wild and reckless in her life. Being the nice, reliable, bleeding-heart owner of an art gallery, she was far more the type you'd expect to run off to join the Peace Corps than to shack up with some guy. Yet here she was. And, frankly, she'd never been happier.

"Are you sure you don't want to come with me today?" he asked. "Free food."

"No, I don't think so," she said, slowly shaking her head, capable of no more movement than that. "I need to float in the pool and recuperate."

"From?"

"From you."

"From us, you mean," he said, nuzzling her throat. The sensation of his slightly stubbled jaw against her skin made her quiver with helpless appreciation. God, she loved the feel of this man, the taste of him, the power of him.

But she hadn't been joking. They'd made love so often, in so many exciting, wild ways, that she figured she should remain motionless for hours, just to regain her strength.

"You go do your being famous stuff, and I'll just nap."

He laughed softly. "You still don't believe I'm famous?"

She hadn't, at first, being someone who paid absolutely no attention to any kind of sports. So of course she had not recognized the championship-winning quarterback, or ever even heard of his name, not until he'd told her last night.

"I believe you," she admitted. "The way women fall over you was a tipoff." Though, of course, his incredible looks—thick, dark hair; dreamy brown eyes; powerful, rock-hard body—could also have explained that. "And the gushing casino owners were, too." Though, of course, his obvious wealth could have had something to do with that. "But there's really no other way to explain that group of college guys who tried to carry you across the lobby last night, unless you're the world's oldest frat pledge or your tastes are a whole lot more varied than you've let on."

He reached over and cupped her breast, reminding her of just how much he appreciated her woman's body. "Don't ever question my tastes."

"So who are you pledging? Alpha Alpha Alpha?" she asked with a giggle, because the man was the definition of that word.

"Very funny."

"Okay, okay. Just remind me—is football the one with the big, round, orange ball or the pointy triangular ball?"

"You're hopeless," he said, running his fingers gently through her hair. He'd admitted that her red hair had caught his eye from across the casino the night they'd met, and that he'd been hoping she would cross his path. Funny that she'd ended up cheering on one of her friends at the craps table where Nate was laying bets much larger than her own. Funny…and lucky.

"Sorry, the only sport I enjoy is croquet. I'd kick your ass in croquet."

"I don't doubt it."

And she didn't doubt him, not anymore. She'd been skeptical at first. After he'd told her who he was, laughing at her shocked expression when he admitted most of the rest of the world would have recognized him on sight, she'd checked him out on the internet. Yeah, he was a pretty big deal. Which just made her wonder even more why he'd spent the past three days glued at the hip to her.

Of course, their hips did match up very nicely. As did all their other parts.

She shivered with the thrill of the sensual memories. Noticing, he dropped a powerful arm across her waist, pulling her close, as if to warm her. But frankly, when Nate pulled her against his smoking body, she didn't get warm—she got hot. Luckily, the opulent suite at one of the most exclusive five-star hotels on the strip was nicely air conditioned.

"I'm becoming addicted to you," he whispered as he leaned closer to scrape his lips along the edge of her ear. He nibbled on the lobe, breathing hotly down her neck.

"I can't move," she said, groaning even as she laughed at how utterly relentless he was.

"You don't have to. Just lie there and enjoy."

Good lord. The man was insatiable. But when he began to kiss his way down her body, she certainly didn't protest. Instead, as his warm mouth reached her breast and his lips covered her nipple to suck deeply, she merely groaned.

"I love these," he mumbled as he moved to suckle the other.

"I'm so glad," she purred, her strength returning as a different kind of energy began to pour through her.

He continued to caress her breasts, squeezing lightly. The tension within her increased, the pleasure exponentially so, and she arched toward his strong, warm mouth. Her breasts had always been sensitive, and when he drew on them like that—*oh, God, like that*—she thought she might climax merely from the sensation of his lips and his masterful tongue on her skin.

He kissed her between her breasts and then descended down her body, lavishing attention on her sensitive skin. She quivered beneath him, holding her breath as he explored her, inch by inch. She was almost crying by the time he stopped at her belly, dipping his tongue into the hollow, nibbling her hipbone, his very breaths hitting all her pleasure sensors.

"Nate, please," she cried, begging him to go further, to give her the kind of dizzying climax he could so easily provide. The man's mouth was perfect for smiling, but even more perfect for oral sex, at which he'd already proved himself a master.

"Please what?"

"Please use your mouth on me." She had no shame with him; he removed every thought in her head but the need to climb ever higher. "Make me come."

"Greedy girl."

She twisted beneath him, and finally he continued to move down. By the time his jaw brushed against the soft curls between her legs she was on fire, a live wire of sensation.

She *was* greedy. With him she was a different woman. With this amazing stranger she was a completely sensual being, in tune with every ounce of pleasure she was capable of achieving.

"Oh, God, yes," she groaned when he moved his mouth right where she craved it and stroked her with his tongue.

He groaned himself as he tasted her, eating her into a mindless frenzy. She'd had oral sex before, but never with someone who seemed to totally get off on giving it. Nate devoured her as if he was starving, his warm tongue licking into her, making love to her, before he returned to her clit and got serious about bringing her to orgasm. The intensity of the sensation was shocking, overwhelming, and she began to shudder, bucking up toward his mouth.

And then the pressure erupted into a warm sea of waves that rolled through her, relentless as a tide, bringing utter satisfaction. She cried out, stunned by the power and perfection of her release. Nate moved up her body, kissing the sound right off her lips, before the pulsing delight had ceased. And then he was inside her, riding it out with her.

"I can't get enough of you," he growled as he plunged deep. "The minute we stop, I fantasize about starting again."

"Ditto," she muttered, shocked that he could have made her so wet, so ready for him again, when they'd made love more times in the past three days than she had in a year. But every inch of her was attuned to him, welcoming his massive cock, loving the heat of it, the thickness of it, the way he bored into her as if he was an explorer claiming her for his very own.

She'd always viewed sex as a journey toward orgasm, not realizing quite how remarkable the trip itself could be.

"I've never experienced anything like this."

"Neither have I," she admitted.

"Don't leave tomorrow."

She tightened her legs around his hips, arching up to take his deep thrusts. "I have to."

"Why don't you come to Miami with me?"

She laughed, but the laughter melted into a helpless groan when he plunged again.

"Come with me."

"I'm going to," she said, deliberately misinterpreting. And a few moments later, when he reached his climax, angling his hips to give her just enough pressure where she required it most, she did exactly that. Heather let out a little scream as she fell off the ledge into pure sensory delight all over again.

"Come with me," he demanded, staying on top of her, kissing her jaw, her nose, her lips.

She considered it. There was her shop—her employees *were* very reliable. Her schedule—she could always change Friday's dentist appointment. Her houseplants… *screw the houseplants*. Her parents—they were so in love, they probably wouldn't even notice she was gone. Her father was capable of taking care of her more-than-a-little-flighty, dreamy, irresponsible mother.

"My place is right on the beach," he told her as he brushed his stubbled cheek against hers. "You can walk out my door and be in the surf within a hundred steps."

Oooh, tempting. April in Vegas was very nice, but it definitely wasn't a beach in Florida.

"Give me a chance to think about it," she said, sorely tempted to say yes. But she wanted to get away from him, to evaluate the situation rationally. Right now, with his naked body entwined with hers, all gleaming with sweat, both of them so sated and delirious, was no time to make any major decisions. And skipping off to Florida with a football-playing superstar was a major decision.

"Okay," he said. "I have to do this charity thing and press junket. But promise you'll consider coming while you're lying by the pool, and we'll talk about it tonight?"

"I promise."

"And if you decide no, be warned—I can be very persuasive when there's something I really, *really* want."

NATE REALLY, *REALLY* wanted Heather.

He wasn't sure why, couldn't say how she'd embedded herself so deeply in his psyche, but it was true. He'd become addicted to her over the past three days.

It wasn't just that she was beautiful, with her long, red-gold hair, pale green eyes and slim figure. He also enjoyed her sense of humor and her kindness, and was attracted to her spirit. She was natural, with not a fake bone in her body, unlike most women he met. Definitely unlike the one he'd planned to marry.

The difference between gallery-owner Heather Hughes and Felicity Monroe, his bubblegum-pop-singing ex-fiancée, was like the difference between a five dollar bottle of Chianti and Pernod Ricard Perrier-Jouët champagne. They might both get you drunk. But one would leave you with a headache and a sour taste in your mouth, while the other left you feeling pretty uplifted. The fact that he'd ever proposed to Felicity embarrassed him. He was just glad she'd eventually revealed her real, vicious personality behind the sweet facade she'd shown him at first.

As he stood in a crowded hospital corridor, he tried to force memories of Felicity out of his mind. He was always willing to help out good causes, and didn't regret saying yes to today's appearance at a new wing of a children's cancer center. The press conference afterward would be a pain, but hopefully it would go quickly.

Then he could return to the hotel and Heather.

"So, Nate, do you have any comment about Felicity's news?"

Nate, who'd been squatting down to autograph a football for a cute five-year-old, tensed, recognizing reporter-tone. He finished signing the ball, tousled the kid's hair and rose. Before him stood a middle-aged man whose eyes sparkled with excitement. *Nothing beats digging into other people's dirty laundry.*

"The press conference is happening later. If you have to ask about ancient history, save it until then. This is about the kids."

Not even curious about what his ex's news might be, he began to walk away. But another guy with a press label on his jacket stepped in front of him. "Nate, will you support your child?"

Nate's whole body went rigid. *Child? What the hell?*

"Haven't you heard about Felicity's interview on *The View* this morning?"

"I don't know what you're talking about," he said, desperate to get to a private spot to contact the team's press office. He'd intentionally kept his phone off for the past few days, being focused on Heather. That must be why he hadn't heard about this yet, though, obviously, word was spreading.

The reporter didn't let up. "She announced her pregnancy, naming you as the father. Felicity said that when you found out, you dumped her. She mentioned a lawsuit for breach of promise."

Christ, was that even still a thing?

"And said she'll sue you for child support."

"This is crazy," he said, swiping a hand through his hair.

"How do you respond to the allegations?"

"I deny them," he snarled. "We broke up…" He was about to yell *because she cheated*, which she had. But he instead fell silent. Felicity was very popular right now, and the team's PR reps had thought it best that the breakup appear mutual.

"Because you're just not ready to be a father?"

"That wasn't it." He glanced around for an organizer, hoping someone could get rid of the human piranhas who loved to nip at the heels of any celebrity, especially one who'd recently dumped a VH-1 goddess. No one was nearby. *Figures*.

"Is it because of the redhead?"

Jaw tight, he responded, "What redhead?"

"You've been seen all over town this week with a mysterious red-haired woman named Heather."

Nate reached for the guy's lapel, ready to grab and shake him, but sanity prevailed. "She has nothing to do with this."

On cue, the other one leaped in with the same question. "Is she the reason you abandoned Felicity and the baby?"

There is no baby, he mentally screamed, absolutely certain it was true.

Yes, he and Felicity had broken up only a month ago. But before that, she'd been on tour in Australia. Before *that*, he'd been wrapped up in the playoffs. Plus, their relationship had been on the rocks, since he'd suspected—correctly—that she was cheating on him. The point was, they hadn't slept together since Christmas. If she was four months pregnant, the world would have known about it by now, or she'd have told him during their ugly breakup scene when she'd begged him to take her back.

This was a publicity stunt, it had to be. And on the off chance she *was* pregnant, the baby wasn't his. The father was probably the married music producer she'd screwed around with.

"Look, this is the first I'm hearing about any of this."

"Did you have an affair with Heather and break Felicity's heart?"

It was like talking to a damned wall.

Whatever happened, he had to protect Heather. She was a private person, one who valued her reputation as a business owner. The first priority was to get the spotlight off her.

"This redhead you keep harping on is a stranger,"

he said. "I met her a couple of days ago, we hung out and that's it."

"So there was no love triangle between you, her and Felicity?"

"Definitely no love triangle," he said, keeping cool. "There's no love between me and Felicity, or me and anybody else. The redhead is a chick I picked up in Vegas. She's a nobody."

He mentally apologized to Heather. He'd explain it to her later, when they were safely inside his gated house in Miami.

Unfortunately, he immediately realized, that wouldn't work.

She couldn't come with him, not now. Bad enough that he lived in the spotlight because of his own fame. Felicity positively thrived on it. She'd milk this as much as she could, for whatever twisted reasons she'd come up with for announcing the pregnancy and naming him as the daddy.

The press would watch his every move, and would notice if Heather traveled with him or if she showed up at his place. She'd be thrust into the spotlight, and she would hate it.

As much as he dreaded letting her go, they had to separate so he could deal with this. It might drag on for a while, but the truth would come out eventually. Fortunately, since his dad lived in Albuquerque, they could hopefully manage a few visits.

Trying to decide how to explain all of this to Heather, he returned to the hotel late in the day. Entering his suite, he called, "I'm back." No answer. The suite was utterly silent. "Heather?"

When he walked into the bedroom and saw that none

of her clothes were draped across any of the furniture, his heart skipped a beat. He opened the closet door, finding it empty of all her belongings.

"Heather?" he called again, willing her to answer.

Again, silence. He was completely alone.

Then he saw the note propped up against the lamp.

He grabbed it, certain something major had happened, and she'd bolted. While he didn't wish anyone ill, he couldn't help but hope there had been an emergency back home and her departure had nothing to do with his tabloid drama.

Nate—I had to leave. Emergency at home. No lie.

"Thank God," he muttered, though guilt speared him the moment he said the words. His relief was short-lived, however.

I guess the timing works out well for you, considering what the reporters said when they cornered me at the pool.

"Oh, shit."

Glad to hear we were both on the same page about it being a fling. Makes me feel better about having to leave like this.
Thanks for everything.
—The nobody

Nate read the note twice, his eyes returning to those final words. *The nobody.* That's what he'd called her to the reporters. His unthinking comment—meant to spare her from the public eye—had hurt her and then sent her running. She might sincerely have had an emergency, but he doubted she'd have left without even a call if she hadn't been targeted by the press.

His first instinct was to go after her, to fix this right now. Hell, maybe she could use his help with her emergency.

His second—more rational—instinct was to let her go. He could be in for a long, ugly fight, both in the media and, possibly, in the courtroom. A public relationship with Heather would only make things worse for both of them.

Besides which, she was apparently in the midst of a crisis. What kind of asshole would he be to heap more stress into her life by drawing the bloodsucking flies of the paparazzi to her door, as his presence would surely do?

He couldn't. He just couldn't do it to her.

"Damn it, Felicity," he muttered, wishing he'd never laid eyes on his ex, who'd fooled him and the world into believing she wasn't the vapid, shallow, vain woman she truly was.

Now he'd met a real woman—a smart, sexy woman he knew he could fall for. And, for her own good, he had to let her go.

At least for now.

2

Ten Months Later

BEING A BRIDESMAID was supposed to be fun. Being the maid of honor at the wedding of someone you truly loved even more so.

But when the bride was your mother, who'd been widowed due to the death of your adored father less than a year ago, *fun* wasn't the word to use. Heather would prefer to listen to a chorus of six-year-olds singing that song from *Frozen* on a 24/7 loop than hear her mom say one more word about her upcoming Caribbean wedding.

"Are you sure you've got enough sunscreen?"

"I'm sure," she said, even as she fantasized about getting a bad case of sun poisoning so she could bail on the wedding.

"And a hat and cover-up? That tropical sun is so strong!"

"Two hats, three cover-ups, a few long-sleeved shirts. Know where I can find a burqa?" Her tone was as calm and even as her expression. Frankly, she was starting to congratulate herself on both. She'd gotten pretty good at hiding her true thoughts.

"Smarty-pants," her mother said with a laugh, not reading anything into Heather's mood. How she couldn't realize that her daughter was a steaming ball of emotion most of the time was beyond her.

Seriously, her mother was a smart woman, but she appeared to have no clue that Heather, who'd adored her dad, was heartbroken about Amy's whirlwind romance, engagement and destination wedding. In two days, they and twenty other friends and family members would fly to Miami to board a private yacht, with a crew of ten. Five days of sailing would take them to Barbados, where her mother would marry a rich stranger whom Heather hadn't even met.

Her fault, she supposed. She'd evaded every possible meeting, never imagining anything would come of the romance. It was too painful for her to even think about her mom dating anyone. Not because she didn't wish her happiness, but because it was just too soon. Heather wasn't over her father's unexpected death at only fifty-one. How could her mother be?

Short answer: she wasn't. Amy Hughes had always been the queen of denial. Heather feared she was now denying herself the chance to grieve.

She'd told herself her mother's fling with an Albuquerque businessman was none of her business. Her mom had always been, as her father had called her, a flibbertigibbet—flighty and joyful. That described her mom to a T. But she also had a huge heart full of love, and she craved it in return. She was a vibrant, pretty fifty-year-old. Of *course* she'd want to be in love again.

"Still, did it have to be so damn soon?" Heather mumbled.

"What was that, honey?"

"Nothing," she said as she parked the car outside the country club where tonight's engagement party was being held.

It seemed dumb to have an engagement party a week before the wedding. But the bride and groom had wanted all the guests to meet on neutral ground before they boarded the yacht where they'd be stuck together for five days.

Heather could only list a few things she'd less look forward to doing for five days, including getting parts of her body waxed or listening to her dad's old Bee Gees collection.

"I'm so excited that you're finally going to meet Jerry," Mom said as they exited the car. "You'll love him."

Maybe. As soon as she was able to stop crying for her dad.

"I just hope his son will approve of me," her mother added.

Heather stopped mid stride. *"Son?"*

"Yes, he has one son. Didn't I mention that?"

"No." Jesus, she was now going to have a stepbrother to go along with the stepfather? Only in her mother's flibbertigibbety world would something like that not have come up before now.

"Well, to be fair, baby girl, you haven't been very interested in hearing about Jerry or the wedding."

"No, I guess I haven't." Then, because she simply *had* to say something, she added, "Mom, are you sure about this?"

Her mother kept that smile pasted on. Heaven forbid they have an honest conversation that pierced the happy bubble. Heather's greatest fear was that when the bubble inevitably burst and her mother allowed herself to truly grieve for what she had lost, she might be stuck in a marriage with someone she didn't love.

"What do you mean?" her mother asked, continuing to play the game they'd been playing since the day of her father's funeral, when her mom had declared she was too young to wear black and had put on a pink dress. *Put off until tomorrow what you can't deal with today.* That was Amy Hughes's motto.

"I mean…it's awfully soon."

"Yes, but I married your father after only nine months and look how well that worked out. I may have only met Jerry six months ago, but I'm even older and wiser now."

Heather hadn't been talking about how long her mother had known this Jerry dude, but rather about how long it had been since Dad's death. But of course, Mom realized that. She just didn't want to talk about it. Meaning Heather had to zip her lips and paste on a smile, or force the issue and risk her mother exploding into tears right before the party.

Heather might be ruthless when it came to running her business, but she couldn't be toward her sweet-natured mother. So, with a sigh, she said, "Just promise me this party has an open bar."

"Well, of course it does, honey."

Of course. The groom had boatloads of money, after all. Jerry what's-his-name was a real estate developer and had enough cash to ensure his new bride would never want for a thing for the rest of her days. Unlike

Heather's dad, the English teacher, whose heart had always been bigger than his bank account.

She kinda already hated Jerry on principle.

"There he is," her mom said, squeezing Heather's arm. "And that tall young man with him—well, that must be Nathan."

Heather stiffened, unable to prevent the reflex. Ever since her aborted romance with football superstar Nathan Watson last year, she tensed whenever she heard that first name. Which made it imperative to keep away from sports channels throughout the winter. But even that hadn't been enough—she'd also had to avoid any tabloid-type news for a while, considering he'd been embroiled in a baby-daddy scandal with his pop-star singing ex for months.

How silly she'd been, hoping he would get in touch with her at some point. Her note had been brief and cryptic, surely he would be curious, perhaps even apologetic. But there'd been nothing. Not a single word. Which said everything there was to know about what he'd really thought of her.

She was, indeed, a nobody.

She forced her mind off of Nathan—his handsome face, the amazing three days they'd spent together—focusing instead on her mother's romantic drama. Her own was in the past and there it would remain. Nate's utter silence proved that.

"Here we are!" her mother called to the two men who stood on the front patio of the club, almost nose to nose, appearing deep in an intense and possibly heated conversation.

Both men turned toward them, the salt-and-pepper-haired one stepping to the edge of the patio, into a pool of exterior light. Heather's stomach churned as she noticed the fact that he was good-looking, well-built and eyeing her mother adoringly.

Before she had a chance to process that, though, the taller, younger man walked up to join his father. And the world stopped spinning. Or, at least, her little corner of it did.

"No," she mumbled in disbelief. "It *can't* be." Fate wouldn't be so unkind as to thrust her biggest regret into her path at the same time she had to deal with this crazy wedding.

Fortunately, her mother had kept walking, so she didn't overhear Heather's words. She was left to stand there on the sidewalk, gazing up at the patio, at the very familiar man whose whole body was rigid with tension. "Nate? Is it really you?"

He froze, staring down at her, recognizing her at once. Even as his jaw unhinged, she could read his emotions as they washed over his face, one after the other—surprise, perhaps pleasure, regret and then anger. She understood each of them. Because she felt all those things, too.

Nate looked the same but for a few lines on his face that had probably been caused by the stress of this last year. They didn't lessen his attractiveness one bit, serving only to make him more mature and handsome. Which was why, even as her stomach churned with tension, her heart was fluttering and her panties were getting a little damp.

She'd been telling herself for ten months that what they'd shared had only been lust—just hot sex, easily forgettable. But seeing him again now, she couldn't lie to herself anymore. She'd been well on her way to falling in love with the man. His silence had crushed her, especially after her father's death, when she'd begun to evaluate her own life, to realize how fleeting it could be, and how desperately she wanted someone to share it with.

Someone like Nate.

And then, finally, he spoke. "You have *got* to be kidding me. How much worse can this whole thing get?"

Heather had never realized shock and embarrassment could segue so immediately into fury. So much for love and happily-ever-after. Who the hell did he think he was to ask her to come back to Florida with him, then tell the press she was a nobody? To ignore her for months? And now to act as though he'd been injured by having to run into her again? What a prick.

"So nice to see you, too, superstar," she snapped as she strode up the steps to the porch.

Nate thrust a hand through his thick, dark hair. He rubbed his eyes and sighed heavily before finally facing her head-on.

"I'm sorry, Heather, that wasn't directed at you. I was just caught off guard."

"You and me both."

Her mother and the older man she assumed was his father had been watching them, their eyes rounded. Her mom said, "Nathan? I'm Amy, and I'm so happy to meet you."

Nate offered her a very tight smile in response.

"Am I correct in thinking you're acquainted?" she added.

"We've met," said Heather.

Nate nodded. "We, uh, got to know each other last year during a trip to Vegas."

"What a small world!" His father stuck out his hand to her. "I'm Jerry. So nice to finally meet you, Heather."

"Hello Mr....Watson." God, she'd barely even listened when her mother had mentioned Jerry's last name. If she'd been more attentive, would she have been a little more prepared for tonight? Doubtful. The surname wasn't exactly a unique one. Besides, who could possibly prepare for such a catastrophe?

Heather shook her future stepfather's hand. That much, at least, was easy, since her whole body was shaking.

She'd imagined running into Nate again, visualizing a hundred ways it could happen without her having to stalk him at a Thunder game. Yet her imagination could never have come up with this situation.

Bad enough having to run into her fickle ex-lover on the very same night she felt as if her personal life and world were imploding. Worse, though, was that he was so obviously furious about it, apparently having hoped to never lay eyes on her again.

She had, many times, told herself she wished she'd never met him. Right now, she actually believed it.

"This must be quite a surprise then," the groom said.

"Surprise. That's one way to put it," said Heather.

Sick might be another way.

Still, queasy or not, her heart was fluttering as she recalled that last morning in bed at the hotel. Nate had been so attentive, so sexy, so adoring, as if he had meant it when he'd said she was becoming his addiction.

That seemed, sometimes, to have been her last truly happy moment. By that afternoon, everything had gone to hell. First, she'd been cornered by some obnoxious reporters about the rumors of her being the "other woman" in a celebrity love triangle. Before she'd even had a chance to process those rumors, or what he'd supposedly said about her—*a nobody?*—she'd gotten the call that Dad was in the hospital, in critical condition.

She'd barely made it home to say goodbye. He'd died the next day. And every moment since, she'd been busy trying to hold herself together, and her mother, too. All the while, she'd wondered if she'd already met the love of her life and if he would end the silence and come find her.

She'd wanted that, desperately. Wanted a once-in-a-lifetime love like her parents had had. Wanted a man who would adore her the way her dad had adored her mom. She'd fantasized about having that kind of love with Nate.

Boy, had she been wrong.

"Isn't this fun," her mother said, clapping her hands together and looking absolutely delighted. "You two are already friends...and now you're going to be siblings!"

Oh, my God. Nate Watson, the lover she'd almost flown off to Florida with last spring was about to become her stepbrother.

Heather suddenly couldn't breathe. How could her world have turned so completely upside down so fast?

Before she could think better of it, given the presence of the parents, she said the only thing that made sense right now.

"Fuck my life."

NATE DIDN'T SAY the words, but he echoed Heather's sentiment. Because, damn, how could he be expected to deal with his father's crazy, impulsive engagement to someone Nate totally believed was a money-grubber...

when said money-grubber was the mother of the woman he'd lost his head over last year?

It really was her. Heather Hughes. In the flesh. He hadn't believed his eyes at first, but once she'd spoken and he'd heard that soft, sexy voice, he'd been unable to deny it.

The beautiful woman hadn't changed since he'd last seen her. Well, maybe a little. He'd certainly never seen her with such a dark frown on her face. The faint shadows of sadness he noticed in her eyes were unexpected, too.

Had he contributed to that sadness? He knew he'd probably hurt her by never reaching out after their fling in Vegas. He'd had her number and could have used it at any time. Unfortunately, his life had become so ugly he couldn't bring himself to do it. There'd been tabloid reporters digging through his trash, private investigators following him and lawyers subpoenaing his medical records. Just crazy crap for months, right through his first losing season.

The experience had changed him, hardened him. Frankly, he hadn't been fit company for anyone, much less a woman. Which was one reason he hadn't ever tried to reach her.

The other reason was…well, he'd been burned by Felicity. Badly. As much as he liked to think Heather was different, in truth, he'd only been with her a few days. He'd begun to question every decision he'd made— including the decision to ask a near stranger to come home with him. His judgment could have been screwed up about her, too. Maybe she'd been aware of who he was all along. Women constantly pretended to feel things they didn't feel when it came to men with money. He should know.

So, he feared, should his father, who'd been married three times and messily divorced twice.

And was about to embark on adventure number four.

With his ex-lover's mother.

Heather was right. *Fuck my life.*

"Shall we all go inside? I'm sure the other guests have already arrived," Amy said, choosing to pretend she hadn't heard her daughter's muttered obscenity. She tucked her arm into his dad's and added, "We're going to have a lovely party." Her comment sounded more like a threat than a promise.

Nate was left to escort Heather, who was glaring at him as if she'd scraped him off the bottom of a shoe. Not even one of hers, maybe a garbage man's shoe. Or a…a dogcatcher's.

"I can't believe it's really you," he managed to mutter as they walked into the club and followed the sounds of laughter toward a nearby banquet room.

"Yeah, seeing you here is the highlight of my decade, too."

Sarcasm. He wasn't used to it from her, but he had to admit he kind of enjoyed it. Sharp, sassy Heather was someone he hadn't met before, and he found her incredibly attractive.

"We should talk."

She glanced at him out of the corner of her eyes, which sparkled and snapped with emotion. Anger, he'd venture to guess. "Funny, I can't imagine a single thing I want to say to you."

"Then I'll talk and you can listen."

Whatever else happened—if he succeeded in getting his father to reconsider this insane marriage to her mother or not—he needed to apologize to Heather. He had to explain why he'd said those things about her and why he'd dropped completely out of her life. He only hoped she'd believe he'd done it to protect her. After that, they could go their separate ways.

The Nate of a year ago might have considered making another play for her, seeing if those sparks were still there and if the two of them had a connection that could last. The newer, more jaded Nate knew better. Considering he believed her mother was out to marry his dad so she could suck his bank account dry, he had to wonder if Heather was a chip off that block. Even if she weren't, once he broke up this insane engagement, she'd never want to speak to him again. So, yeah. Best to apologize and then forget all about her.

Inside the crowded room, where the bride and groom were getting lots of kissy-huggy greetings from a bunch of people he didn't recognize, he and Heather headed, by silent consent, toward the bar. Nate noticed the attention Heather got—God, who wouldn't stare at her? Two thirtyish men who'd been standing at the bar talking real estate both lowered their drinks, exchanged *Whoa, look at that one!* glances and offered her very warm smiles.

Nate had no claim on her, none whatsoever, but he still had a serious urge to smash a jaw or two.

The one in the blue suit snuck a quick glance at Heather's ass. *Definitely two jaws.*

He shouldered his way between Heather and the nearest jerk, keeping his back to them, blocking her from their view.

The bartender, however, he could do nothing about,

and the young guy was already flirting with her as he asked, "Would you like the signature drink for tonight's event? Sex on the beach?"

Nate felt a little sick, thinking of next week's beach wedding. "We'll each have a dry martini, two olives for the lady. Three for me," he said, remembering her drink of choice.

She frowned, but didn't correct him, apparently needing the alcoholic fortification more than she needed to put him in his place. Nodding her assent to the bartender, she didn't even look at Nate as she muttered, sotto voice, "Let's just retreat to opposite corners and pretend we don't know each other."

"That'll work well on a yacht," he said.

"Maybe I'll just push you overboard."

"I'm a good swimmer."

"Into a school of sharks."

Her curmudgeonly attitude coaxed a laugh from him. It sounded rusty. Unused. "You'd have to add a lot of chum to the water to get a whole school of great whites on my tail."

The bartender slid her drink over, his fingers deliberately brushing hers on the glass as she took it.

Nate gritted his teeth.

"Thanks for the tip," she said as she lifted her martini and sipped it. "I'll start gathering dead fish guts now."

He sighed heavily. "Speaking of guts—you hate mine, huh?"

"Well, you certainly didn't make me feel like you were any happier to see me just now."

"I was," he admitted, his tone low, the admission startling even himself. "Heather, I have to explain some things."

"Don't bother. I got the message. I happen to be fluent in silence—it's one of my favorite languages. And yours was pretty deafening." She smirked, then sauntered over to a table in the back corner, obviously thinking she'd had the last word.

Nate followed, unable to prevent his attention from traveling over her long, wavy red hair. His hands tightened as he remembered the feel of that silky mass twined around his fingers. Her green sheath dress did amazing things to the body he'd worshipped for three days straight, and the gentle sway of her curvy hips as she walked soon had him panting.

Whatever had happened during the past ten months, one thing was sure: he still wanted her.

Heather didn't chat with anyone, obviously wanting to sit in a corner, alone, to lick her wounds. But he couldn't let it go. If he didn't succeed in getting his father to change his mind, they were going to be stuck together on a yacht for several days. He had to clear the air before that happened.

He sat beside her at the empty table, getting right to the point. "I was trying to protect you."

She blinked and finally peered at him. "Excuse me?"

"What I said to the reporters—about you being a nobody."

She tossed her head. "Oh, that. No big deal."

Her tone was as breezy as a woman who'd just told her husband she didn't mind that he'd forgotten their anniversary. I.e., blasé, but not quite hiding a promise of retribution.

"It was a big deal and I apologize. I hated myself the minute the words came out of my mouth, but you have to understand…"

"You had a pregnant girlfriend to mollify?"

He squeezed his glass. If the glass had been of lesser quality, it might have shattered in his hand. "God, no."

"I guess I was the only one on the planet who was unaware you were involved with a pop star when we met."

"That she *had* been my girlfriend is true. But we broke up before I met you." He put a hand on her shoulder, urging her to believe him. "I swear, I'm not a cheater."

She stared into his eyes, searching for answers. He hoped she recognized the truth. Whatever else he might have done in the past year—and he wasn't proud of some of his actions—he'd never betrayed anyone in that way.

"Okay," she finally said with a nod. "So you didn't cheat."

He didn't breathe easily just yet. "Nor did I dump a woman who was pregnant with my child."

"Yeah, I heard DNA tests proved the baby wasn't yours."

"The media reported that *eventually*," he muttered. "But not until I'd been raked over every coal Kingsford ever made."

Her tense posture finally relaxed a little. "I'm sorry."

"Not your fault."

"Not apologizing. Empathizing. I'm truly sorry you went through all that." She licked her lips, then, her voice a little softer, asked, "Were you disappointed? I mean, when you found out that the baby wasn't yours?"

Nate barked a harsh laugh. "There was no chance in hell he could have been mine. I was sure of that from day one."

Her pretty brow furrowed. "But, I mean…"

"She got pregnant two months after we stopped sleeping together. I guess she figured because I was a football player I couldn't count all the way up to nine."

Heather's green eyes rounded. "You mean, it was all a lie? She knew all along it couldn't be yours?"

"Yeah. Pretty sick, right?"

"How did she ever believe she would get away with it?"

"Felicity always gets what she wants, and never imagined she couldn't get me back. She assumed she could get me into bed soon enough for me not to question who'd fathered her baby." He offered Heather a jaded smile. "When her private eye spotted me with you in Vegas and told her he thought it looked serious, she panicked and called the press."

"That evil bitch!"

Yeah. She was. Not that the world had seen her that way, even after the paternity had been proven. He was still the guy who'd broken poor Felicity's heart and hadn't stood by her after her, uh, mistake. He was also the subject of her last hit song, *Broken Promises*, an honor he would have happily gone without.

The married producer was out of the picture. No matter how furious Nate had been, he'd never outed the affair to the press. So the baby-daddy was now a big mystery. With no other face or name to dog, the tabloids remained focused on him, to hell with biology. Or decency.

"Anyway," he said, thrusting off the ugly mental images, "it all started to break that day in Vegas. You were already getting caught up in it, and I knew the paparazzi would be on you, making your life miserable. That's why I said what I did, to throw them off track.

I apologize for how it sounded, and how it must have made you feel."

She remained silent for a moment, considering. Eventually, she nodded. "All right, I can accept that."

As for the rest—why he'd never called her—well, that was a long story, one not suited to their surroundings. Besides, he wasn't sure he could explain it without sounding like an asshole who feared he could never trust another woman. He wasn't a misogynist. He still liked and respected women. But the trust thing was going to be hard to get over.

So all he said was, "I stayed out of touch because my life's been pretty screwed up ever since."

She downed her drink. "Join the club."

Hearing the pain in her voice, he asked, "They didn't—I mean, nobody from the tabloids ever came after you, did they?"

"No. I escaped their radar." She fished an olive out of her drink with her long, slim fingers and popped it into her mouth, the movement as graceful as it was sexy.

Damn, he was still so affected by this woman. He had to drag his eyes away from those lips as he asked, "Then what do you mean? What happened? Was it something about the emergency you mentioned in your note that day?"

"Indirectly, I guess." She nodded toward the happy couple, who were dancing to a big band number on the otherwise empty dance floor. "Essentially, *that's* what happened."

"So you're not happy about this, either?"

She shook her head, and a rush of relief flooded him. He had been worried Heather would support the romantic lunacy when, in fact, she might actually be an ally.

"Thank God," he said, lifting his own drink and tossing back a mouthful. "I thought I was gonna have to break up this wedding all by myself."

Shock widened her eyes. "What do you mean?"

"I mean, I flew here today to convince my father how crazy this whole thing is. We've been fighting about it all day."

"Fighting…"

"He's such a romantic. A sucker for a pretty face. Two out of three of his former wives have swindled him out of fortunes. My dad can't see clearly when it comes to women."

"Swindled?"

"What's that old saying? Marry in haste, repent at leisure. Believe me, his accountant always repents," he said, thinking how lucky he had been that his own romantic misadventure hadn't actually led down any aisles other than in a courtroom. "Desperate, middle-aged women see the name and the dollar signs and can't resist trying for the brass ring. He falls for it every damn time."

Heather stared at him for a long moment, her eyes flashing. Her whole body had grown rigid, and her mouth opened and then snapped closed, as if she were trying to control herself.

Which was when Nate remembered exactly who he'd been referencing as a desperate, middle-aged woman.

"Oh, crap, Heather."

"My mother is no swindler." She launched from her chair.

He rose, too. "I'm sorry, I didn't mean…"

"Yes, you *did* mean. You think my mother's marrying your father for his money?"

No backing off that now, and no way to say it nicely. "She wouldn't be the first bored divorcée to want what a rich man can give her."

Heather gasped, drawing a hand to her chest. Her fingers pressed so hard they left red marks on the pale, creamy swell of her cleavage. It was as if she were trying to hold her heart in place, as if he'd wounded her.

He was so out of practice talking to women. He'd lost his charm, and tonight, it seemed, even his tact. Maybe it was her nearness that had loosened his tongue, and his own recent history that had made his words so bitter. Maybe the martini he'd just consumed—and the two he'd had earlier—had contributed, too. In any case, Heather appeared as furious as a tornado.

Without another word, she swooped her nearly empty glass off the table. To his shock, she tossed the contents— liquor, melting ice, one olive—right into his face.

"Stay away from me, Nate Watson," she said, her whole body shaking. "Or I swear to God, I will pitch you off that boat right in the middle of the Caribbean and laugh while you drown."

3

DURING THE FLIGHT to Florida two days later, Heather was fortunate enough to be seated far away from Nate. That wasn't too difficult, since there were about twenty other people in their group. Jerry had invited a few of his employees, and her mother had asked a bunch of her friends to come, plus Heather's two cousins and their wives. Other than a brunch yesterday, she hadn't had to see Nate, and she'd managed to avoid saying much to him there.

When they arrived in Miami, stretch limousines waited to take them to a beachfront hotel where they would spend the night before the cruise got underway the next morning. Heather was supposed to ride in a limo with the bride, groom and best man. Like that was gonna happen.

Intentionally dawdling in the terminal, she missed her car and got into the last limo. In it were six of Jerry's friends she didn't know, including two guys with beer bottles in hand.

"Hey, Red! You're slumming back here with us today, huh?"

"Ha-ha," she said, wishing she'd been faster so she could have hopped in with her mom's friends or her cousins.

"So what did Mr. Quarterback do to deserve a drink in the face the other night?" asked a blond man wearing a Hawaiian shirt. "Don't tell me—you lost a bundle on his last game, too?"

"Not a football fan," she said, tucking herself closer to the side of the car. He didn't get the hint, edging closer.

"I don't blame you after last season. Talk about suckage."

"I bet *lack* of suckage was the problem," said the other one with a suggestive eyebrow wag. He was dark haired and attractive—and he knew it. "He was missing Felicity's mouth."

Now she *really* wished she hadn't played these car games. Not just because the guys were drunk and obnoxious, but because she didn't want to hear about Nate or his pop-star ex.

"I'd be happy to be on the receiving end of her suckage!"

"And I'd be happy to be accused of being her baby-daddy."

"Excuse me," Heather said, elbowing the blond. "This car is huge. Do you have to sit on top of me?"

He grinned and blew out a breath fragrant with onion rings and beer. Ugh. "You can sit on top of me, if you want."

"Go away, or you'll get worse than a drink in your face."

"Touchy, touchy," he said, hands up, palms out, playing the role of injured party. Typical man.

Fortunately, another occupant, a middle-aged woman, saw what was happening and shoved her way down the long seat to squeeze in between Heather and the guy. "Sorry, honey. Can't take the bears out of the cage."

"Or the dogs out of the pen," she muttered.

She tried to ignore them as the men continued to rag on Nate's season. She wanted to tell them to shut up, not liking to hear anybody ripped apart. But a tiny part of her kept hearing the words "swindler" and "middle-aged divorcée" echoing in her head, and she decided Nate could fight his own battles.

The fact that he didn't realize her mom had recently lost her husband of thirty years made no difference. Because he hadn't bothered to find out before shooting off his mouth. His words had stabbed her right in the heart. She'd give anything for her mom to be merely a happy divorcée if it meant her father was still alive somewhere in this world. So, no, she was nowhere near ready to forgive him.

She was, however, able to spare a moment to wonder what had happened to the charming, sexy guy she'd gotten to know in Vegas. Nate had changed so much. Every time she saw his handsome face, it was dark and forbidding. He barely spoke to anyone. The tension between him and his father was thick enough to swim in.

He was not the same man she'd fallen for. And while that made it easier to resist him, it also broke her heart a little.

Enough with the broken heart, she told herself. He didn't want her heart, and he seemed pretty anti-love-and-romance in general, judging by his assumptions about this wedding. For the past year, since Dad's death, love had been one of the foremost things on her mind.

She wanted a once-in-a-lifetime love. Nate Watson did not.

The car stopped more quickly than she'd expected, and she was the first to hop out when the driver opened the door. To her surprise, they were not parked in front of a hotel, but rather in the circular driveway of what seemed to be a private home.

"Mansion," she clarified, eyeing the sprawling white house, three stories tall, that was framed by swaying palm trees and lush flowering rhododendrons. Marble columns lined the expansive front porch, and the massive door stood open, with waiters on either side of it, holding trays of cocktails for the guests.

"Yeah, this is Jerry's son's place," said the woman from the limo. "We're dining here before going on to the hotel."

Oh, brilliant. She was going to have to spend the evening wondering if he had a servant on guard to follow her mother around to make sure she didn't steal anything.

Heather politely declined a tour of the house. Instead, she veered straight through to the back patio, which overlooked the ocean. And there she felt her tension ease.

It was, without a doubt, glorious. The views of the beach were stunning, extending as far as she could see in either direction. The crashing of the waves onto the white sand a few dozen steps below was almost lyrical, lulling in its regularity. She could happily have pulled up a lounge chair and spent the night right here. Or the entirety of the upcoming cruise.

"It's something, isn't it?" asked Steve, her cousin.

He stood nearby with his wife, Becca, who was five months pregnant.

His brother Josh replied, "Sure is. I wonder if he could score us some tickets."

"He seems to be a nice guy," said Steve. "I bet he would. Especially if his little *sister* asked him."

"For God's sake, stop gushing," she snapped, the word *sister* hitting her like a punch. "He plays a game for a living. He hasn't brought peace to the Middle East or cured a disease. He runs around on grass like a ten-year-old, and gets paid an obscene amount of money to do it. It's disgusting."

"Actually, I didn't start playing until high school. So maybe I run around like a fifteen-year-old?"

Heather groaned when she realized Nate had walked up in time to hear her comment.

Hell. Last she'd seen him, he'd been inside, talking to the caterer, doing his best to pretend there wasn't a party going on. He might be Mr. Charming for the press, but she'd noticed his sullen mood. If she weren't so unhappy about this wedding herself, she'd slap him for being such a downer.

Of course, he *had* offered up his house for this party. She honestly couldn't figure out his motives.

Stiffening her spine, she turned to face him. "Okay," she said, not relenting, "so you get paid an obscene amount of money to run around like a teenager. Is that better?"

"Sure."

"Come on, Heather, there's a little more to it than that," said Josh, frowning at her for her rudeness.

"Occasionally I have to throw the ball, too," Nate said.

"Yes, I'm sure that's so challenging."

"Ask my body. It's been challenged."

She couldn't resist casting a quick glance over him. He wore a dress shirt, open at the throat with the sleeves rolled up, and khakis. He looked casual and totally at home here in Florida. And hot. So damned sexy. No shirt could mask the broadness of his shoulders, and the fabric strained against his muscular arms. His waist was still narrow, his hips lean. Every inch of him was in perfect physical condition.

God, the dreams she'd had about that body. Those hands. Those lips. That big cock that had given her such pleasure. The man had ruined her for other lovers. She hadn't had one since she'd last seen him.

Maybe she'd remedy that on this cruise. Pick up some young island guy who'd ply her with rum and cool off all her hot urges. She imagined letting loose and proving to herself—and Nate—that he no longer had any claim on her. And, having freed herself from the physical longings, maybe then the emotional ones would disappear, too. She could go back to Santa Fe with a clear head and a clear heart, ready to meet Mr. Right, having purged herself of all longing for Mr. Oh-So-Wrong.

Finally realizing she'd been staring, she cleared her throat. "Well, I guess people who don't have the intelligence to hold an important, meaningful job have to find something to do."

Becca gasped. So did Josh's wife, Tracy.

"Yes, how lucky I am to have found a job that requires no brains, drive or dedication." He smirked. "And how goes the art biz? Changing the world one brilliant paint splatter at a time?"

Another gasp from the onlookers.

"I do all right." She gestured toward the house. "And

you certainly seem to be well compensated for your aches and pains."

"I am. In fact, I'm hoping to invest some of that compensation in art. I hear you're the expert. Maybe you could help me out."

Oh, hell no. "I doubt we have similar tastes."

"You sure about that?"

"I'm not into black-velvet paintings of card-playing dogs."

Beside her, Josh coughed. Nate's eyes narrowed, but his lips twitched the tiniest bit. "Gee, and I thought you'd skipped the tour of the house."

Had he been watching her from the minute she'd arrived? "I can use my imagination."

"That's not necessary," he said, reaching for her arm and sliding his own through it. "I'll take you on a private tour."

"Not interested," she snapped, trying to pull way.

But he had a strong grip and they were surrounded by wide-eyed witnesses. She couldn't very well shove him over the patio railing onto the beach below, as tempting as that might be. Which was why she gave up and let him pull her inside.

As soon as they were clear, she snapped, "Let me go."

"No. You've been avoiding me. We need to talk before we leave on the cruise with all these people."

"You can't just…just pull me around."

"Would you rather I pick you up and sling you over my shoulder like a sack of potatoes?"

"If you do, I swear to God, I'll kick you in whatever spot my feet are close enough to reach."

He didn't loosen his grip. "Try it and I'll tie you up."

That threat sent excitement surging through her, not fear. Nate was so different now—not the sweet, sexy lover she'd come to know in Vegas. There was an edge to this Nate, a darkness. It scared her a bit. Mostly, though, she found it arousing.

Stop it. He's a jerk. You're not falling for him again.

"Come on," he insisted, dragging her toward a large, sweeping staircase that curved gracefully to an upper level.

They marched up to the landing above. He continued prodding her toward the end of the hall and a pair of closed doors. She had the feeling she knew what was behind them. When he pushed them open, showing her a huge master bedroom with a wall of floor-to-ceiling windows and glass doors, she stopped dead.

"Forget it."

"It's the only place we can have some privacy," he said. "I just want to talk."

Really? Was that all he wanted to do? Because talking was the one thing she did not want to do with him. Using that bed, however… *No!*

He moved behind her to shut the double doors, locking them to ensure they wouldn't be disturbed. "I have lost my ability to speak when I'm around you," he said, staring down at her, his brown eyes narrowed and his brow furrowed. "I keep putting my foot in my mouth."

She looked away. "No kidding."

"I didn't mean to say those things about your mother the other night. I don't even know her."

"If you did, you'd realize she's honest and kind, and definitely not a swindler."

"Bad choice of words." He walked toward the patio doors, gazing out at the ocean and crossing his arms over his chest. "I shouldn't have made snap judgments about her."

"No, you shouldn't have."

"I...apologize."

"Gee, you're using that word a lot with me this week."

"Too often." Still not looking at her, posture stiff, almost angry. "And I apologize for that, too. I...haven't been myself."

No kidding. He was a very different man. But she would have sworn that when they were bantering earlier, the real Nate, the sexy charmer she'd met in Vegas, was still lurking in there somewhere.

He glanced at her over his shoulder. "Have you resigned yourself to the fact that there's nothing to be done about this wedding?"

Heather hesitated, torn between the truth and her desire to keep a distance between them. Finding any common ground could be dangerous, could make her start to care about him again, more than she should. Besides, the sting of his comments about her mother hadn't entirely eased, despite his apology.

"They're grownups," she replied with a shrug. Unable to resist, she came closer, drawn by the magnificent views. From up here, she could see farther out into the ocean, enough to catch a glimpse of a far-off ship heading up the coast. She couldn't imagine waking up to this every day. "This is so lovely."

"You should have been here to see it ten months ago."

Without warning, he reached up and brushed her hair off her cheek. Heather sucked in a breath, shocked by the warm pleasure that washed over her at such a simple graze of skin on skin.

She'd missed his touch. She'd missed everything about him.

"Heather…"

"Don't," she said, shaking her head and stepping away. Because missing wasn't enough. There was such a thing as self-respect. Not to mention self-preservation. "It's too late."

"I know that." He moved toward her, close enough that she could feel the warmth of his body just inches away from hers. She felt the magnetic pull of it down to her very bones. "But I can't help myself. I've got to touch you."

Before she could reply, he'd reached up and cupped her face in both hands. And then he was kissing her and sanity disappeared.

NATE HAD BROUGHT her up here to talk, only that, needing to make amends for the shitty things he'd said about her mother the other night. That he'd believed them to be true at the time—and was still on the fence about Amy's motivations in marrying his father—wasn't the point. He never should have said such things to Heather.

But seeing her here in his bedroom, standing in a beam of sunlight that illuminated streaks of spun gold through her red hair, he'd simply been unable to resist kissing her.

She didn't resist, either. After that one shocked flare of her eyes, he'd covered her mouth with his and she'd responded with the same need.

Ten months disappeared. So did all the negative crap he'd been dealing with. He'd never understood what getting lost in a kiss meant until he met her. And he welcomed being lost again.

She tasted the same—that unique, spicy-sweet flavor that belonged to Heather. The fruitiness of the drink
she'd been sipping was still on her tongue, making her
that much more delicious. He plunged his tongue deep
into her mouth, exploring and savoring her.

She met him stroke for stroke, thrusting her tongue
against his, soft, warm, wet. She twined her arms
around his neck and held him close. Her delicious body
melted against his, and Nate growled in the back of his
throat, all his male genes recognizing her, wanting nothing more than to again possess her.

Sinking his hands into her hair, he turned her head
so he could go even deeper, intent on sampling every
single bit of her. He moved his hands down her neck,
reaching around to the zipper at the top of her dress.
The zipper made the faintest of sounds as he slid it
down—the only thing audible, other than their own
shared breaths.

He tilted her head again, taking more of her hot,
wanton kiss as he pushed the dress off her shoulders.
It was loose and soft, a pretty, flowery thing that had
drawn his eye again and again on this morning's flight.
She'd ignored him, but he'd been able to see, think of
and want nothing else but her.

The dress had been beautiful on her, but it looked
even better on the floor.

He ended the kiss so he could draw away and stare
down at her, smiling at the sight of those beautiful bare
breasts—she hadn't been wearing a bra. Her nipples
were so pretty and pebbled, revealing her arousal. Not
that he wasn't already fully aware of what she wanted.

He moved his mouth down her throat, kissing her,
biting lightly, breathing in her fragrance. "I couldn't

think of anything else on that plane today except how much I wanted to join the mile-high club with you," he admitted as he reached for one breast, cupping it, tweaking the nipple with his thumb.

A throaty laugh left her mouth.

"God, I want you," he admitted. "Not a day has gone by when I haven't thought about you."

"You could've fooled me."

He heard the tension in her voice, but also felt the pliant longing of her body. She was trying to stay angry but couldn't manage it. And neither could he.

"Heather…"

"Shut up, Nate," she said, twisting her fingers in his hair as he moved down to her breast. "Don't talk. Let's just communicate the way we do best. With sex."

"Fine by me," he said before licking that saucy nipple. When she gasped, he covered it and suckled her, continuing to squeeze and toy with the other one.

She was shaking, shuddering, and had to lean back against the glass door. Nate continued to move down her, tasting her, looking for changes to the feminine form he'd memorized last year. He found none—she was still absolutely perfect.

He dropped to his knees, kissing her belly as he drew her panties down her bare legs. Moving lower, he rubbed his lips over the soft curls of her crotch, breathing on her, inhaling her. Heather groaned and shifted her legs apart.

He flicked out his tongue, searching for that pretty little clit, knowing just how to make her crazy. Heather gasped and jerked toward his mouth as he lavished his attention on her, getting off on the musky taste of her, the sweet, womanly way she smelled.

He reached up and grabbed her hips, arching her toward his hungry mouth, sliding his tongue down between her lips. Heather twined her hands in his hair—not to push him away, but as if needing to hold on for dear life while he fucked her with his tongue. She lifted a leg and draped it over his shoulder, giving him better access, and he plunged deep, licking into her and then going back to her clit to give her more of what she needed most.

It took less than a minute. She shook, cried out and tightened her grip on his hair, rocked with an orgasm. Her legs trembled and she leaned on the door for support.

He slowly rose, tasting his way up her body, noting the flush of color on her skin, hearing her pants as she reacted to the powerful climax. And when he was again facing her, he kissed her deeply.

"I want you, baby," he said.

"Then take me," she begged.

He reached into his pocket and grabbed his wallet, retrieving a condom. Heather was already working his belt and pants open, and when her soft, cool fingers brushed his cock, he thrust into her grasp. She squeezed him, smoothed her hand over the tip of his erection and then lifted her fingers to her mouth to lick off the moisture. The sight of his seed on her lips was enough to send another gallon of blood racing to his cock. If he couldn't get inside her this instant, he was gonna go into cardiac arrest.

Despite his shaking hands, he somehow managed to sheathe himself and stepped toward her. Heather lifted her leg, and he caught it in his grip, pressing her back against the glass. He found his way unerringly to the hot core of her, sinking his cock into her tight pussy with slow deliberation that belied his frantic need.

He'd dreamed about this too much to rush. He wanted to savor every bit of her. The slowness enabled him to fully appreciate the pleasure every single one of his senses was being bombarded with by the beautiful woman in his arms.

"Nobody else ever felt this good," he said, losing himself, inch by inch, in the tight heat of her.

"I know."

"I've lain in that bed, dreaming of you, fucking my own fist more times than I can count in the past year."

She groaned and squeezed him, deep inside, eliciting a groan from him, too. "I'll admit, I invested heavily in some toys."

He laughed, which was crazy since he was having hot sex with a woman he'd fantasized about for months. But that's how it was with Heather.

Suddenly, needing her to hear it, he said, "There hasn't been anyone else. Not since you."

Ten months of celibacy. It hadn't been intentional… but he suspected his subconscious had known he wouldn't find satisfaction with anyone else. Not as long as Heather was buried so deeply in his psyche. The months apart had only made her more beautiful, more alluring in his mind. But none of those images and fantasies could compare with the woman in the flesh.

She looked up at him, those green eyes wide and more than a little surprised at his admission. Nate held his breath, wishing he'd said nothing, because she hadn't responded in kind.

It killed him to think of her with anybody else, whether he'd been around or not. He had no claim on her, had in fact hurt her, but he seriously wanted to put his fist through the wall at the very idea that any other man had been where he was now.

Finally she put him out of his misery. "Same here."

He let out a relieved breath. "I realize I didn't have any reason to expect…"

"No, you didn't." She ran her tongue along his earlobe, biting hard enough to make him wince. "But you may have ruined me for other men."

"Same here."

"I ruined you for other men?"

He laughed. "Shut up."

"Okay, but only if you shut up, too, and finish what you started."

"Yeah," he said. "Actions are better than words."

He lifted her other leg, desperate to find his way a little bit farther into her until he was completely buried. She wrapped her thighs around him, and he gripped her by the hips as he drove even deeper.

Heather cried out, raking her nails down his spine and squeezing him tightly, inside and out. And, at last, he felt as though he was in the right place again, back where he was supposed to be. The anger, disappointment and frustration of the last ten months fell away and he let himself do nothing but *feel*.

In Heather's body, in Heather's arms, nothing else mattered.

He pulled out slowly and thrust in again, greedily taking more as she arched to meet him. Their bodies were slick with sweat. He tightened his grip on her hips, and her eyes flared in excitement. She twisted her fingers in his hair, almost painfully, as hot passion snapped between them.

Nate tried to maintain control. But the electricity between them sizzled as she began to lose hers. It was too good, too intense, too hot to resist, and he could no longer take it slow and steady.

"Gonna go hard now."

"Do it."

That was all the permission he required. Burying his face in her throat, he pulled out of her and then thrust to the hilt. She was mumbling something—*Yes, yes, yes*—and matching his every movement. Together they thrust wildly, he giving all he had to give, she taking it and begging for more. Until at last he hit the cliff and came with a long, shuddering moan.

Heather was still holding on, her arms around his neck, her legs around his hips. She kissed his earlobe, traced her tongue down his neck, murmuring soft sounds of satisfaction.

He wanted nothing more than to walk over to his big bed, toss her onto it and stay there for days. But even now they could hear voices downstairs and outside. A house full of guests was waiting for them, probably already wondering where their host had disappeared to and why he'd been gone so long with the maid of honor.

"I guess we can't stay here and do this all night," he said with a sigh of disappointment.

"I guess not."

He slowly let her down, and she bent to pick up her dress and panties, noticing the glass behind her.

The color fell out of her face. "Oh, my God, you don't suppose anybody could have seen us, do you?"

"Nah, the angle's wrong."

"I should hope so. Can you imagine?"

"Would it matter? We're not sneaking around, are we?"

She shook her head as she reached around her body
to zip up her dress, shoving her feet into her sandals
at the same time. "No, sneaking around won't be necessary. This was a one-shot thing. I'm not into stepbrother romances."

He closed his eyes and shook his head, hating that
image. "Way to kill a mood, Red."

"There is no mood. It's done."

"You really believe that was it for us?"

"Yes, I do. We have to get on a small boat tomorrow..."

"That boat is not small, believe me. It's almost two-
hundred-and-fifty feet long."

She shrugged, obviously not truly envisioning it. He
understood—the thing had to be seen to be believed.
The charter yacht was crazy extravagant, costing more
for a week than most houses, but nothing was too good
for his father's bride.

"It'll feel small with two dozen other people on it,
watching our every move. In Vegas, we could do what
we wanted because we were completely anonymous.
But everything's different now."

She walked past him toward the adjoining bathroom,
and he followed. As he cleaned up and got his clothes
back into place, he watched her eye her messed-up hair
in the mirror. She blew out a frustrated breath and then
grabbed his comb to try to fix it. But she was obviously still filled with a nervous type of energy—maybe
stress—as the truth of what they'd just done hit her.

"You're gonna make yourself bald," he said, taking
the comb from her hand and gently working through
the tangled strands for her. Her hair was silky, thick
and soft. He hated that he was fixing it for her to go
downstairs to interact with other people, when what he

wanted to do was strip her naked and stay in bed with her for the next week.

She stood there and let him. "Thank you."

"You're welcome," he replied, putting the comb down and then turning her to face him. "You ready?"

"For?"

"For the dinner party from hell?"

She laughed softly. "I suppose."

"For a maid of honor, you don't sound excited about the festivities."

She licked her lips, rubbing her hands up and down her arms, as if chilly. "I'm just…this has been hard for me."

"It's going to be a lot harder once those two realize what a huge mistake they've made," he said, trying to keep things even. Because, though he questioned her mother's motives, he also questioned his dad's. His father had married out of sheer loneliness more than once, to his great regret.

"Maybe," she said. "Or maybe they're really in love and will live happily ever after."

Nate couldn't help rolling his eyes and huffing out a disdainful grunt at that idea.

"What, you don't believe in true love and happy endings?"

After the year he'd had? "No, Red, I really don't."

She licked her lips, pivoting away from him toward the sink, where she busied herself washing her hands.

He'd said the wrong thing, something she didn't want to hear. For a moment, he half regretted his answer but it was the truth. He had never believed in fairy-tale romances, and the last year had made him stop believing in romance altogether.

Sex? Hot, wild screwing up against the door the way they'd just done? Yeah. He believed in that.

But love, soul mates, happily-ever-after? Honestly, he didn't believe they existed. That didn't mean he wasn't enjoying himself with Heather and couldn't envision them continuing this white-hot affair. But love…that word wasn't in his vocabulary.

"At least you're honest about it," she murmured.

"Only way I know how to be."

She gestured toward the bedroom. "So this was…"

"Fantastic? Something I want to repeat many, many times?"

A faint hint of color flushed her cheeks. "It was just sex."

"Great sex."

"Yes. But just two bodies, doing what comes naturally."

No, it hadn't been that at all. Not to him. Heather wasn't interchangeable with any other woman—she was the only one he wanted. For now. But that didn't equal love. Right?

"Look, let's not debate it or put a name on it," he said. "We have chemistry, Heather. Let's leave it at that."

Her jaw was tightening. Her eyes narrowed. "Chemistry."

He drew her close, putting his hands on her ass and pulling her up on her toes so their bodies lined up the way they were meant to. "We're good together. Let's have fun while we can."

He bent to kiss her. She jerked her face away. Which was when he realized how seriously wrong things had gone.

"Admit it, you want me as much as I want you."

She shook her head slowly and backed out of his

arms. Her rigid posture told as much of a story as the sheen of moisture he saw in her eyes.

"Being good together and having fun isn't enough for me, Nate. Maybe it was last spring, in Vegas. But I'm not the same person I was then. My life has changed, and I've learned some drastic lessons. I want something different now." She drew in a deep breath, and slowly released it. "So I'd really appreciate it if, once we get on that boat, you stay away from me."

"You've gotta be kidding."

Her chin went up. "No, I'm not. I'm finished, Nathan. *We're* finished. I want you to leave me alone."

Their stares met and locked, both of them breathing heavily with passion and anger. He waited, certain she would temper that, change her tune, but she didn't say another word.

He couldn't believe she was really pulling this, and wasn't sure what she wanted him to say. That he had wedding bells ringing in his ears, and thought the two of them could go off and live in a fairy castle? Honestly, these days, he was just happy to be with someone who not only made him hot, but also made him laugh. He liked her, a lot. He wanted to be with her. Why wasn't that enough for now?

Whatever the reason, whatever she claimed, he was aware of one truth: sexually, she wanted him as much as he wanted her. Her mouth might say one thing, but her body said another. He certainly wasn't going to force her to admit it, but sooner or later she would. Especially since they were going to be together for the next week in some pretty romantic, sensual settings.

"Okay, Heather," he finally said, "have it your way." Then he smiled, full of confidence. "But something tells me your way is going to last no more than twenty-four hours." He reached out and brushed a strand of her hair off her cheek. "You want me, babe. You know it, and I know it. And once we're stuck on that boat, and you can't hide away and pretend otherwise, you're going to admit it to both of us."

4

NATE HADN'T BEEN kidding when he said the yacht was huge. Heather had been struck into utter silence when the limos dropped them off at the port and she realized they'd arrived at their destination. When she'd first viewed the massive, graceful craft, she'd mistaken it for a small commercial cruise ship.

It was anything but. The *AnnaLucia* was the visual definition of luxury. If Jerry had spent less than a half million on this cruise she'd eat her flip-flops.

That was probably more than her father had earned in a decade. *Toto, we are not in Kansas anymore.*

Honestly, she wasn't sure what she'd expected. Maybe something like submarine-barracks type accommodations, with bunks for all the single ladies, of which she was one.

Instead, the ship boasted fourteen bedrooms. As the maid of honor, and the bride's daughter, she had her own. Nate did, too, and the bride and groom shared the luxurious master stateroom. The remaining eleven rooms were divided among the other guests, and everyone swore they'd never slept in such comfortable beds.

The common areas were magnificent, boasting plush leather furnishings, thick carpeting and mahogany paneling. There was a seawater swimming pool on deck. Nearby was a six-person Jacuzzi. And a bar manned by a guy who made the best mojitos she'd ever tasted.

If the warm sunshine, smooth, crystalline waters and poolside bar weren't entertainment enough, you could hang out in the game room, complete with every game system known to man, or the small movie theater with films from all over the world. The on-board hair salon didn't come with a hairdresser, but the mirrors and lighting were fabulous. There was even a spa with a trained masseuse. The two chefs provided delicious, gourmet meals in the centrally located dining room, and the crew was always on hand to help satisfy any craving an onboard guest might have.

Except, of course, the sexual craving that had been gnawing at Heather's bones from the moment she'd realized her stateroom was two down from Nathan's. And both were very lush and private.

"You're halfway there," she mumbled as she headed up to the pool on the third day of the cruise. "You can make it the rest of the way."

Sure she could. She was woman, hear her roar and all that.

Truthfully, though, she had to admit, if he'd put much effort into it, he could probably have her purring instead of roaring in no time. Telling herself she wanted more than he could offer was all well and good. But seeing his gorgeous, muscular body in his swim trunks on deck every day, and noting how the other women all drooled over him, too, was playing hell with her self-control.

If a sexier man existed on the planet, she'd yet to

meet him. Nate, with his windblown dark hair, his ruggedly handsome face, those broad shoulders and thick arms, and rippling six-pack of muscles, was absolutely sex on a stick.

She still wanted him, desperately. No island hookup with a random guy was ever going to be a good enough substitute. He had been totally right about how she was going to feel during this cruise.

As it turned out, though, he'd didn't try to seduce her. He had made his desires clear at the house. More than once she'd caught him watching her with desperate want, and he'd offered her intimate smiles that invited her to let down her guard. But he hadn't so much as touched her in the past two days.

It was a message: If a move was to be made, she'd have to be the one to make it. He'd drawn a line in the sand, wanting her on his own terms and wanting her to admit how much she desired him. Nate was holding out for a no-strings fling like they'd had in Vegas and was confident she would give in.

The fact that she no longer wanted that would sink into his head sooner or later. She hoped.

To help ensure it, Heather went out of her way to convince him she wasn't interested. If the rest of the guests wondered why she sniped at him so often, or why he zinged her right back, they at least minded their own business. Hopefully nobody realized it was pure, sizzling sexual tension that made them act as if they couldn't stand the sight of each other. But, underneath the bickering, she sensed his amusement—and his confidence. If he were a betting man, she imagined he'd have laid money that before this cruise ended she would be back in his bed.

If *she* were a betting woman…well, she wouldn't bet against him.

"No! It might feel good now but will only hurt more when he's had his fill and moved on," she told herself as she walked up the stairs toward the bright sunshine. Wanting to take advantage of the gentler, early-morning sun, she was skipping breakfast, figuring she'd grab something later.

"There she is! How'd you sleep, Heather?" called Hank, one of Jerry's employees, who managed an office in Arizona.

Hank was the obnoxious blond from the limo ride. He wasn't as bad as he'd seemed at first, probably because he'd nursed a hangover and seasickness the first two days of the cruise and had cut way down on the drinking. Right now he seemed sober and happy, sitting poolside with a smear of white on his rather large nose.

"Fine, thanks," she said as she stripped out of her clothes, down to a hot-yellow bikini, and sat on a lounge chair near the railing. "Feeling better today?"

"I'm finally sober," he admitted, appearing sheepish. "I plan to stay that way for the rest of the week. Don't know what I was thinking on the flight down here— except that I'm scared to fly! I'm just glad Jerry's a great, understanding boss."

So she kept hearing. Everybody sang Jerry's praises, especially when she was in earshot. Perhaps they'd noticed she wasn't exactly cuddling up to her new stepdaddy. She was never rude or the least bit unfriendly. But she didn't go out of her way to spend time with the man, either.

"Your loss, bro. But hey, Red, you can count on me to keep your whistle nice and wet."

That came from the dark-haired one, Tony, who had lived down to all her initial impressions of him. Cocky and on the make, he had his eye on Heather. Absolutely the only reason she spoke with him was because she knew it drove Nate nuts.

Like now.

Nathan had just emerged on deck—in time to hear Tony's comment—and he glowered at the other man who was floating in the pool. She wasn't sure if it was because Tony had picked up on Nate's unwelcome nickname for her or that his comment had been so suggestive. Either way, it didn't bode well for a peaceful morning sunbathe.

"Why don't you put some clothes on before you burn yourself to a crisp?" Nate snapped at her, confirming her suspicion of his mood.

"Why don't you mind your own business?"

As if. "Aren't you afraid red skin will clash with that carrot-red hair?"

She gritted her teeth. Her hair was not orangey, the jerk. But she managed to feign calmness. Reclining in the chair, she closed her eyes and ignored him.

"I mean it, you're going to fry."

"I marinated myself in SPF 50 before I came up."

"Your nose is getting freckles."

"They're adorable!" said Tony.

She didn't open her eyes to witness Nate's reaction. She didn't have to—she would swear she heard a low growl from the man.

"No, they don't," he finally said. "They look like the skin cancer fairy sprinkled some magic dust on you."

Ouch.

"You should really go inside."

"If you're so worried about the condition of my nose, why don't you change colognes?" she muttered. "That stuff you wear is killing me."

Tony snorted with laughter, but before she could congratulate herself, she heard a familiar voice cry, "Heather!"

Crap. Her eyes flew open and she saw that her mom and Jerry had just come outside. Her mom was wide-eyed with shock and not a little anger.

Nate smirked. Ass.

"What on earth has gotten into you?" her mother asked, walking over to confront her as if she was a kindergartner who'd stolen another kid's Go-Gurt. "Where are your manners?"

"Sorry," she muttered. "But he did start it."

"Did not," said Nate.

We do *sound like a pair of six-year-olds.*

"He said my hair was orange."

Nate cleared his throat. "I said I was afraid she was getting too much sun."

Jerry, who had come over to join her mom, laughed. "You'll have to forgive Nathan, Heather. He's just not used to being a big brother. I'm sure he'll get the hang of it."

That was enough to make her blood boil. Brother? God, this was beyond ridiculous. Nate didn't appear much happier at the description and was frowning at his father. Finally, for the first time in days, something they agreed upon: they could never have anything resembling a sibling relationship.

"Well, if you can't start getting along, I'm going to get one of those Trouble T-shirts I've seen moms put on their kids," said her mother. "It's one giant shirt with two arm holes, and the kids have to wear it together until they stop fighting. I'm tempted to put the two of you in one!"

Heather swallowed hard, and Nate stepped away to study the horizon. The idea of being bound up together was a little too dangerous for either of them to contemplate. Especially in front of family.

"I hope you can manage to get along this afternoon on the island," Amy added. "And to make sure of it, I've paired you up for the scavenger hunt. You'll have to cooperate and work together if you want to win a prize."

"Oh, good lord," Heather muttered.

At a steady eighteen knots, they were making excellent progress en route to Barbados. They should easily arrive two days from now, in plenty of time for the wedding the following evening. So her mother had been delighted to find out the crew had planned a stop on a private island for a beach picnic and this stupid scavenger hunt.

"What will there be to scavenge on this island, except seashells and sand?" she asked.

"You'll find out," her mother said, exchanging a mischievous glance with Jerry. He kissed her temple and hugged her, as affectionate and tender as only a besotted man could be, and led her belowdecks.

Heather watched them go, swallowing the lump in her throat. Over the past few days, she'd been studying the couple, trying to get a read on their true emotions. While she still believed it was much too soon, and she wasn't nearly ready to give up the memories of her father as her mom's only husband, she couldn't deny the truth. Amy and Jerry cared about each other. A lot. More, they made each other laugh. And laughter was one thing she'd sorely missed hearing from her ebullient mom.

They were happy together. Whether she—and Nate— liked it or not.

Glancing at him, she saw that Nate was watching, too, his brow furrowed. "Didn't anybody ever tell you to stop frowning before your face freezes like that?" she snapped, fearing he hadn't truly changed his opinion of her mother.

"No. I musta missed that lesson when I was learning about the dangers of sun poisoning," he said.

"You are such a sore loser."

"I didn't lose, sweetheart. You're the one who got called on the carpet by your mom."

"Only because you're a liar and didn't admit you said my hair was the color of a carrot."

"I was wrong."

She started to relax, anticipating his apology.

"I should have said radish."

Fuming, she muttered a curse under her breath. But as she said it, she noticed, out of the corner of her eye, that Hank was laughing hysterically. Realizing she and Nate had probably provided quite a few amusing moments for the rest of the passengers at their own expense, she suddenly decided she was ready for her breakfast, after all. And, without a word to any of them, she scooped up her things and went inside, determined to find a way to be super cool when she was alone with Nate on the island.

THE BEACH PICNIC was a big hit. Nate, who had been tense on the boat because he'd been unable to get either close enough to or far enough away from Heather, was finally able to relax. He swam in the ocean, did a little surf fishing, played some volleyball.

Private touring companies apparently used this island frequently, because the crew easily prepared the party, setting up volleyball nets and the grills to cook the food on. They'd had to row everyone and everything over, since there was no dock, making several trips in the two dinghies. But that just added to the adventure of it.

Of course, no matter where he went on the beach, or what he ate and drank, or who he talked to, he was always very aware of that red hair, that white hat and that—God help him—skimpy yellow bikini.

Heather. Jesus, the woman was driving him bonkers.

They'd had all kinds of crazy sex, and yet now, when they were staying on a luxury yacht, which should have been named *The Orgasm* since it was so clearly designed for romance, she treated him like a plague victim.

He had never dreamed she would stick to her guns. Honestly, despite what she'd said in his room the other day, he'd fully expected that she would be unable to resist their chemistry. He'd counted on it, in fact, biding his time, waiting for her to admit she'd been wrong and that they could continue their fling without having to put any more of a name on it than that.

She'd proved him wrong. And he had the blue balls to prove it.

"Okay, everyone, off you go," called Amy, as she and his dad sat at one of the portable tables on the beach. "Each couple has a map with a grid for your part of the island—no fair following anybody else, you have to stick to your quadrant. Come back in two hours. The pair with the most items from their list wins a super prize."

He and Heather stood together—close, but not touching—glancing down at the sheet of paper they'd been given. He could name a thousand things he'd rather do than search for the dumb items on this list. But he had to admit, being alone with Heather somewhere in the island's jungle did sound appealing.

Maybe they'd trip over a snake and she'd be scared and would leap into his arms or something.

Crap. Bad moment to remember he hated snakes. He wasn't scared of them, necessarily, but he'd rather avoid them if he could. Still, if it got Heather to let down her guard and admit she was just being stubborn by resisting their sexual connection, he'd wrestle an anaconda. Hell, whenever he was around Heather, it felt as if he had to wrestle one back into his pants anyway.

"Are you kidding me? How on earth are we supposed to find a pen, pencil or crayon *here*?" she muttered as they began to walk toward the north end of the island—their quadrant.

"Hopefully we'll get lucky and find the old remains of a campsite from a shipwreck survivor who wrote his memoirs while he waited for rescue," he said with a grin, suddenly getting into the spirit of the thing.

She grinned back and wagged her eyebrows. "Or perhaps we'll take a casual stroll toward the surf before we go into the jungle…and I'll grab one out of my bag."

"You'd cheat at a scavenger hunt?"

"Only if it wins me a super-duper prize."

"It's a super-*duper* prize? I didn't hear the duper part. Okay, I'll cheat with you."

Suddenly, they were laughing together. Her laugh

was lyrical, soft and feminine, and he realized it was one of the things he'd most missed about her. Maybe things on the boat were crazy. Maybe in a few days he really was going to have to call her his stepsister. Maybe he was frustrated that she insisted on keeping up this charade that she didn't want him as much as he wanted her. But none of that really mattered right at this moment.

It was a beautiful day. They were on a tropical island. They were totally alone. And he was going to enjoy every damned minute of it.

To his surprise, not only did they find the typical beach-related things—a shell in the shape of a heart, some seaweed—but they also managed to scratch a few of the more unusual items off their list…using the pen she'd sneaked out of her bag. Obviously other tourists had visited the tropical paradise, and they found a Canadian coin, a broken comb and a kid's sand shovel before they'd even left the beach to head inland. When they walked into the shady jungle they added a coconut and a bird's feather to their bag.

"This is a piece of cake," she said.

"You're a born scavenger."

"Speak for yourself. You're the one who climbed that tree and got the coconut."

He lifted the fuzzy round thing, shaking it to hear the milk sloshing inside. "Too bad I don't have anything to open it with—I could go for a drink."

She pursed her lips. "Maybe if we had some rum and pineapple juice to go with it." Holding up the scavenger bag, she pulled out a bottle of water and tossed it to him. "In the meantime, that will have to do."

They walked a little farther with an eye out for some

of the other items, but Nate wasn't really paying attention to the hunt. He was having a lot more fun walking behind Heather, watching the gentle sway of her hips beneath her long, loose peasant skirt. She wore her swimsuit beneath it, but had covered up for their adventure. The gauzy white fabric did nothing to hide the yellow bikini underneath, and he found himself fascinated by the bounce and jiggle of that gorgeous ass.

"Do you hear that?" she asked, suddenly stopping.

He paused. He did hear something. It sounded like a low roar, and it was coming from up ahead.

"Oooh," she said, hurrying toward it. "It's a waterfall!"

He followed her, the low rumbling noise growing louder as they got closer. When they worked their way through a tightly wooded area, and then burst out into a clearing, he understood why.

It was, indeed, a waterfall. A huge, stunningly beautiful one, with cascading crystal-clear water pouring from high above them into a broad pool that glimmered in the sunlight. It was surrounded by trees swaying lazily in the tropical air and was so clear they could see all the way down to the bottom of the pond.

She didn't say a word, she just stripped off her shirt and skirt, kicked off her flat sandals and ran right to the edge. When her toes hit the water, she cooed with pleasure, walking deeper into the sandy-bottomed pool. She resembled some mythical woodland creature with that long red hair and pale, slim body.

Nate stood behind her, watching this stunning woman in this ethereal setting, sure he'd never beheld anything more gorgeous in his life.

"It's wonderful," she said. When the water was at

her waist, she dove forward, emerging a few feet away, droplets glistening on her nose, lips and long red hair.

He wanted to sip that water right off her mouth.

Nate pulled his shirt over his head, kicked off his shoes and dove in after her, gasping at the coolness. It was a refreshing change from the salt water in which they'd been swimming, and he opened his eyes underneath. It was like looking through glass.

He swam under the surface, a few pulls of his arms bringing him to her side, and then rose to stand in front of her. She gazed up at him. He was wet, delicious, glorious. The most perfect thing in the world.

"I want you," he admitted, not even trying to hide his desires. "Thinking you don't want me has been driving me crazy all week."

She hesitated the briefest second and then whispered, "I do want you, Nate. But…"

"No buts." He knew where she was going with that, what she was worried about. He'd done a lot of soul-searching since their conversation in his bedroom, and he was aware he'd probably come off as an ass. Making her believe he wanted her only for sex had been a bonehead move. The truth was, he liked her as much as he desired her.

Maybe it wasn't the happily-ever-after, once-in-a-lifetime love she was hoping for. But it also wasn't merely the lust she'd assumed he was offering.

"Look, we're not exactly the same people we were in Vegas, but we had something pretty good going on." Though it wasn't easy, he also admitted, "I might not be the Prince Charming you're seeking, but I can admit, what we had…it wasn't just physical."

"Really?"

"Really. So can we just forget everyone and everything else for the next hour and enjoy being in this beautiful place together?" he asked, not wanting to waste time hashing it out. Not when they could be doing so many other amazing things.

She hesitated for the briefest moment before lifting her hand and placing it on his chest. Her fingers traced his nipple and tangled in the wiry hair there. His heart was thudding; she had to feel it. His hot blood pounded through his veins as he waited for her answer.

Finally, she took pity and gave him the answer he wanted.

"Yes. We can do that."

5

HEATHER WASN'T A big believer in magic. But this—oh, God, this—was magical.

She had never before experienced a moment of such sensory perfection. The pulsing surge of the waterfall crashing behind them, the caressing embrace of the cool water touching every inch of her skin, the earthy, mossy smell of the jungle surrounding the pool, the eggshell-blue perfection of the sky, the vivid green trees…all her senses were on overload.

But not a single one of those things was as potent—as addicting—as the man who stepped closer and swept her into his arms.

His wet, hard body met hers, and his powerful hands lifted her at the waist. She twined her arms around his neck as their mouths came together in a hot, carnal kiss. His warm tongue tangled and mated with hers, thrusting deeply, his hunger consuming.

The water buoyed her, and she easily wrapped her legs around his hips, not even needing him to hold her. That left his hands free to roam over her body, to reach up and untie her bikini top. When it fell away, his mouth was there to cover her breast.

"Oh, yes," she cried when he licked her wet skin, his mouth ever so much warmer than the water. The contrast was beyond exciting. "More, please."

He complied, covering her nipple and sucking deeply. She felt the pull of it down to her toes as sparks of sensation swam through her. Nate glided his hands down her body, caressing her stomach, her waist, her hips, her ass. Every touch was accompanied by a swish of the water, and the eroticism of it was like nothing she had ever experienced. She couldn't even imagine how wonderful it was going to be when he was thrusting into her, sending waves of water surging against her most intimate, sensitive flesh.

"I've been burning up for you, Heather," he admitted as he kissed his way back up her throat to her mouth. "Every night, I've fantasized about you coming to me."

"I considered it," she admitted. When Nate kissed her lips, her cheeks, her jaw, her eyelids, she wasn't capable of anything except complete openness. No matter the cost. "I thought about it so often."

He didn't ask her why she hadn't come. That would take them beyond their agreement of one hour of carnal pleasure, and neither of them wanted that. Reality would intrude soon enough. For now, there was just this clearing, this pool, this waterfall, this man. This feeling.

Suddenly, his whole body growing stiff, Nate groaned. "Fuck, I don't have anything with me."

"It's okay. I'm on the pill. And since we both already admitted we haven't been with anyone else in almost a year…"

"Oh, thank God," he said, moving to kiss her again.

Knowing he would be inside her, completely, with no barrier at all between them, sent her excitement level soaring.

Their kisses were hot and hungry, their bodies writhing together. Nate tossed his trunks to the shore. He tugged her bikini bottoms off, sending them over, too, and then lifted her up again. She parted her legs willingly, opening up for him, welcoming him in.

His cock was rock hard, hot and wet. As he began to slide into her, she moaned, loving the sensations washing over her. She leaned back, supported by the water, floating as he drove into her inch by inch.

Nothing had ever felt as wonderful as being filled by Nate. He was huge, yes, but their bodies seemed to have been made for each other. She savored the fullness, delighted in it. When he plunged all the way in, hitting her deep inside, she cried out and smiled up at the sky, certain there had never been a moment in her life more blissful than this one.

He didn't move for a moment, both of them enjoying the intense connection.

"I can't believe I haven't sneaked into your cabin and taken advantage of you this week."

"I can't either."

"You thought I would?"

"I thought you might try."

"I was stupid. Stupid and stubborn, waiting for you to come to me."

"Shh," she said, flexing her internal muscles, squeezing him in the way she remembered he loved.

He groaned. Oh, yeah, he liked it all right.

"God, this is amazing," he said as he drew out of her and then slid back in. And then did it again.

The water moved with them, silky smooth, cool, erotic. Every time he thrust into her, a gush of water hit her in all the right places, and her clit almost throbbed as the intensity increased.

He could have sped up, thrust himself into her with mindless passion, but instead he went slow and easy. Deep thrusts followed by short, teasing ones. Light caresses on her throat followed by tweaks on her nipples. She was never quite sure what he would do next, she only knew he would make it feel so damn good.

And he did, loving her, exploring her, making her come and then finally coming himself. Until they were pruned and chilly but still so happy and sated neither of them moved to get out of the pool.

Eventually, though, when she saw that the sun was no longer visible through the opening in the tree canopy above them, she let out a little sigh. "I suppose we should start getting back."

He groaned, but nodded. "Yeah. They're probably ready to send out search parties."

"It wouldn't do to have them find us like *this*," she said with a giggle as she ran her hand down his hard, wet chest. And lower, to his half-erect cock, which thickened the moment her fingers brushed against it.

When he hissed, she pulled her hand away, aware that it would take very little—a kiss, a caress—to get him to forget about the others and the boat. But someone had to be sensible here.

They returned to the shore and pulled their clothes on over their wet bodies. Neither spoke, and despite the warmth of the day, goose bumps rose on Heather's arms. Already, the truth of what they'd just done was flooding her mind with doubts and fears.

Was this the end? Or the beginning? Had they just started something that couldn't be finished in a way that would satisfy them both?

She greatly feared they had. She wanted love. True, once-in-a-lifetime love like her parents had had. And she was already sure she was in love with Nate. She had been for almost a year, even during the long months when he'd been out of her life. When they'd been sniping at each other, when he'd been a jerk and she wanted to push him overboard, she'd still been in love with him.

He wanted sex. Passion, excitement, fun. He wanted her body, and could make her feel things it should be illegal to feel, but had made it clear that commitment, marriage—all that stuff—was not the least bit interesting to him.

One of them was going to get hurt at the end of this. And she strongly suspected it was going to be her.

So she had to try to protect herself, starting now.

"Nate… I don't expect anything," she said.

He flashed that smile that had made her gasp when she'd first seen him last year in a Vegas casino. "Not even a few dozen more orgasms tonight?"

She shook her head slowly, refusing to be teased out of her mood. "I mean, you made yourself clear at your house the other day. I realize you don't believe in all the things I believe in."

"Santa? The Easter Bunny?"

"I'm talking about love. Lifelong commitment."

He tensed.

"You don't believe in those things, and I understand that. I'm not going to make you feel badly about it. But I do want those things. And as much as I enjoy having sex with you, we have to stop." She waved toward the pool. "Let's call that one our last hurrah and let it go."

He gritted his teeth. "Is it always gonna be like this with you? Will you always say no-no-yes-yes-no?"

"I'm sorry, you're absolutely right. I guess my attraction to you always manages to get in the way of my best intentions." She didn't want to be that woman, some kind of tease, and hoped he understood. "I hate wishy-washy people. But the truth is, when we're together and you're touching me, you make me forget everything I know to be in my own self-interest."

Sweeping an angry hand through his hair, he kicked the bag containing their scavenged treasures. "Jesus, Heather, for once can you just admit we have the kind of chemistry most people don't ever experience, and allow for the possibility that we can enjoy that and not feel like shit afterward?"

She heard his anger, his hurt, and part of her softened.

He was right again. He'd pegged her. She did resist, emotionally, anyway, until she couldn't help it and gave in to her deepest desires. And afterward, well, she didn't exactly regret having made love with Nate, but she was always left with a hint of wistful sadness. She always knew that, as much pleasure as he gave her, he wasn't going to give her what she really wanted.

"Yes, we have chemistry. Yes, it's amazing." She bent down, tucking the feather and the coin back into the bag, and added in a soft whisper, "But no, it's not enough for me."

"But it was enough last year in Vegas?"

She drew in a slow breath, hating to even talk about the painful days that followed her trip. Nate, however, deserved to hear the truth. True, he'd changed—but so had she.

"My father died, Nathan."

He frowned as he helped her to her feet. "When?"

"The day after I got home from Las Vegas."

"What?"

"The emergency that I wrote about in my note—I got a call that he'd been taken to the hospital. He had a heart attack. They were planning to do surgery the next morning, but he had another attack during the night. They couldn't revive him."

Nate took a few steps away from her and leaned against a tree, staring at her. "You lost your dad...the next day?"

She nodded.

He put a hand up to his eyes, and shook his head. "And I abandoned you. Didn't even try to reach you."

"It's all right," she said, walking to him, cupping his face in her palm. He covered it with his own, lacing their fingers together. "You couldn't have known. And frankly, for a long time, I was much too numb to worry about whether you were going to call me."

"I'm so damn sorry, Heather."

Tears filled her eyes, but she blinked them away. She hadn't brought this up in a bid for sympathy, but only to make him understand why she wasn't the same girl he'd met last year.

"My dad was the best man I've ever known. He and my mom had a wonderful marriage for thirty years. They adored each other. So I'm sure you can understand why I was so upset about this wedding."

"Of course I can," he said, kissing her fingers. The gesture was sweet and tender, something the old Nate would do. "My mom died ten years ago, and the first time my dad remarried it broke my heart. Especially when it fell apart a year later and the old man was hurt all over again."

Aware of his assumptions about her mother, she said, "I understand things between my mom and your dad better now than I did before this trip."

"Oh?"

"After the scene on deck this morning, my mom finally started talking, being honest about her feelings. She told me the story of how she and Jerry met. I'd never heard it before."

"Dare I ask?" he said with a hard laugh, as if worried they'd met at a strip club or something. Considering she and Nate had met at a craps table in Vegas, she didn't believe he had much room to judge.

"Actually, no. They met in a grief therapy group."

He considered that and then slowly nodded. "My dad's twin sister died last year. She was his only relative other than me."

Her mother hadn't told her that. Knowing he'd lost not only a sibling but a twin made her heart twist for the older man, whom she'd begun to understand a little better. No matter what her opinion of him before, the fact that he'd raised a son as wonderful as Nate—the real Nate—said a lot in his favor.

"I'd been worried that my mom hadn't allowed herself to grieve. I knew nothing about the group. Mom has always been the type to keep a smile on her face and weep silently into her pillow, so she didn't let me see her pain."

"Yeah, I can believe that. She seems like a happy person."

"She is. Anyway, she also made me realize something."

"Which was?"

"She told me that she and Dad had talked over the years about how they loved each other too much to ever want the other to be alone, should the worst happen."

And the worst had most definitely happened.

"If they'd had a bad marriage, she wouldn't have considered the possibility that there could be someone else out there for her. But because she'd had a lifetime of love, she completely believed in it and wanted it again."

His brow furrowed as he dwelled on her words. Then, slowly, he said, "I've read statistics about that. How people who had happy marriages are more likely to remarry after losing a spouse than those who didn't."

"It makes sense to me. My mom did admit that she and your dad got engaged quickly. But I'll be honest, Nate. I believe my mom is totally in love with your dad. And I think he feels the same way."

He was silent for a moment. Heather lowered her hand to her side and stepped away, waiting for him to say something. She steeled herself, fearing his reaction would be negative. Nate might have softened in the past few days, but that angry man who'd fought with his father on the day of the engagement party was still in there somewhere.

Finally, he let out a sigh. "I think you might be right."

She smiled.

"He hasn't been this happy—and at ease with someone—in years. His last two marriages were superficial from the start. He—and his checkbook—always seemed to be on display. Trophies somebody had captured." He smiled crookedly. "Your mom looks at him like he's

Brad Pitt, George Clooney and Prince Charming all rolled into one."

Yes, that *was* how Amy looked at him. It had taken Heather a while to see that, but now her eyes were open.

As for Jerry? Well, he looked at her mother the way her father had. Which was really all Heather needed to know.

"So you're actually okay with this?" she asked.

Another hesitation, and then he nodded. "I guess I am. I'm sorry for the things I assumed about your mother." He swiped a hand through his hair. "Now I *really* feel like a jerk."

"It's okay. You were protecting your father," she said, relief flooding through her. Heather was never going to get over her father's death, nor did she believe her mother ever would, but she was ready to admit that Amy and Jerry deserved their shot at happiness. And the fact that Nate had also come around was a very good thing.

"So," she said, knowing the hard part was still to come, "back to the reason I started this conversation."

"I think I get it."

She was sure he did. But she said it, anyway.

"Losing my father so suddenly really hit home to me, and I realized how fragile and brief life can be. And having seen how happy my parents were together, it made me realize how very much I want that kind of relationship for myself."

Her heart was thudding, and she drew in a steadying breath, not wanting to be emotional about this, wanting him to understand on a purely logical level. Even if she could never be purely logical when it came to Nate.

"I'm twenty-six years old," she continued. "I've played the field, I've dated, I've had flings. Now I want more. And the last thing I need to do is get my heart any more tangled up with somebody who doesn't even believe in the thing I'm chasing."

Love.

Nate had told her he didn't believe in it and didn't want it. She didn't think he'd have said those words in Vegas, and she had to wonder just how horrible this past ten months had been for him to have changed so much. But it didn't really matter. Whatever had happened, he *had* changed.

Maybe he would come around…eventually. She suspected he would, that it was his jaded bitterness talking right now. In a year, he could be back to being that same flirtatious, always-smiling, sexy charmer she'd met, ready to open up his mind and his heart to every possibility.

But she wasn't going to wait around to find out. Her own heart wouldn't allow her to. Because she was already in love with him. If he never changed, if he never loved her back, she would be even more crushed. So saying goodbye was her only option.

"Do you understand?" she asked.

He said nothing, but she saw his jaw clench. Logically, yes, he probably understood. But he wasn't happy about it.

Well, who said they got to be happy?

"I get it, Heather," he told her, his voice low. He cleared his throat, adding, "I wish I could say the words you want to hear right now. If it matters, what we have isn't just about sex."

"I know," she admitted, meaning it. Nate did have feelings for her, she knew that down to her bones.

He just didn't want to.

"Shall we return to the beach?" she asked, blinking away tears.

"Yeah, I guess we should," he agreed.

They picked their way back through the jungle in silence. The afternoon had grown late, it was darker and more shadowy now, their footing was a little less sure. Nate walked a bit ahead of her, holding rough branches and vines out of her way. Heather appreciated the gesture, knowing it was instinctive for him. Everything about him was good, protective, loving. God, she could kill that pop-singing bitch for crushing those innate parts of him beneath her stiletto heels.

Finally they reached the beach and turned to head south. To her shock, Nate reached for her hand, lacing his fingers with hers. He squeezed lightly, but said nothing. The gesture spoke for itself, even if she couldn't quite interpret it.

He let go before they got within sight of anybody else.

It wasn't until they were almost all the way back to the area where they'd had the party that Heather even realized something was wrong. Nate had apparently been equally distracted, because they were within a few feet of the table where Amy and Jerry had been sitting before he said, "Where the hell is everybody?"

"I have no idea." She looked up and down the beach, then toward the treeline. There should be voices, laughter, drinking, music, even yells about the fact that she and Nate were so late returning.

Nothing. It was eerily quiet, except for the steady, inexorable rhythm of the waves softly hitting the shore. The table was still there, as were a few chairs. Some duffel bags and a big cooler were nearby, too, but there wasn't a single person in sight or in earshot.

Suddenly, Nate ran toward the water. "Son of a bitch!"

She jerked her head, wondering what he'd seen. And then she saw it, too.

It was a boat, already far out at sea. Even from here, though, she recognized the graceful lines.

It was the *AnnaLucia*. Their yacht.

Steaming steadily away from the island.

6

NATE SUSPECTED THAT his father wouldn't be happy if he killed his future stepmother, but right now that was exactly what he wanted to do. And he doubted he'd have to do it alone. Because as they read the note that had been left on the table, addressed to them both, Heather looked ready to commit murder, too.

"Are you kidding me?" she asked, blinking and shaking the sheet of paper. Or maybe it was just that her hand was shaking—with fury. "They've abandoned us?"

"Your mother's idea of the Trouble T-shirt, I suspect," he said, reading the note again.

Dear Heather and Nathan—
Hope you had a good time on the scavenger hunt. Your super prize is that you get to spend a few more hours on this lovely island. Surprise—we're leaving you here!

Jerry and I have discussed it, and we have come to realize that the tension between you two is a major obstacle for us. Neither of us wants you to be miserable, and if you can't work out your differences, we honestly don't know what the future will hold. We love you both so much, and don't want our happiness to be the cause of your unhappiness.

Please, for our sakes, and for your own, try to find some common ground and make friends. Love, Mom

PS: We'll be back in the morning. Don't worry, we left you plenty of provisions. Have fun!

They were stranded, just him and Heather, here on this deserted island in the middle of the Caribbean. Civilization was far away, not a single person to interrupt them, distract them, get between them.

Suddenly, Nate's mood began to brighten.

It was crazy. It was manipulative. It was pretty damn pushy. But he was starting to like this whole idea.

"I retract every nice thing I just said about them. Talk about traitors!"

"Well, to be fair, they didn't know you just said a bunch of nice things about them."

Nor did they know he and Heather were a lot friendlier than anybody could have guessed.

"Oh, my God, everyone must have been in on this," Heather said, lifting a hand to her mouth, visibly embarrassed.

"Yeah."

"They probably all just waited until we disappeared into the jungle, then started heading back to the boat."

"Uh-huh."

"Can you imagine how they must be laughing now? 'Let's abandon the troublemakers overnight.'"

Tears appeared in those beautiful green eyes, and he

realized she was genuinely upset. Nate put a hand on her shoulder and took the note away. "We'll be fine."

"How could my mother do this?"

"You tell me. She's your mother."

"She's always been whimsical, overly romantic, but this… God, for all she knows, you could be a crazy rapist."

He barked a laugh. "Your virtue is safe with me," he said, hearing the edge in his voice. Because it was true—she *was* safe with him. He was done pursuing her, trying to make her admit she wanted him. They were stuck here all night, with nothing else to do, nobody else to talk to.

It was, in fact, a golden opportunity. His anger melted away, and he realized he would happily kiss Amy Hughes right now for giving him this chance. Her schemes were going to enable them to sit here all night until Heather admitted what he was certain was true: that they were magnificent together.

So it wasn't exactly what Heather had pictured as a once-in-a-lifetime love. He suspected he could offer her more than she imagined.

Did that mean he loved her? Hell, what did he know? He'd been so fucked over by somebody he believed he'd loved, he had intentionally removed the word from his vocabulary.

But he wanted Heather in every way he could have her. And that had to count for something.

Hearing her talk about her parents, thinking about the way his dad and her mom were with each other… well, he wasn't exactly ready to open a Hallmark store, but he was at least starting to remember that not every relationship was doomed.

Maybe there could be somebody in the world who really cared for him just for who he was, and not for what he could provide. Maybe he could let down his guard enough to open his heart and feel the same way about that person.

And maybe he'd already met her.

"What do we do now?" She glanced toward the western sky. "The sun's going to set soon. It'll be pitch black."

Bending down to search through the bags of things Amy and Jerry had left them, he spotted a lighter. Thankful he wouldn't have to rub two sticks together, he said, "Why don't I start gathering some brush from the trees and I'll build us a fire. It shouldn't be cold tonight, but it'll give us some light, anyway."

Heather nodded, obviously liking having a plan. While he got the wood, she unpacked the bags. Amy and Jerry's scheme had been pretty thorough—not only had they each been left changes of clothes plus beach towels, there were even two sleeping bags. And, to his surprise, a small tent. They could easily sleep on the beach, but it was nice to know they had a tent, just in case.

While he started the fire, Heather opened the cooler and began pulling out food and a bottle of wine. They might be stranded on a desert isle, but the chef had made sure they wouldn't starve.

"Feeling better?" he asked her as she poured two glasses of white wine.

She sipped hers and nodded. "I suppose there are worse ways to be stranded."

"Yeah, Tom Hanks's way was worse."

"And Robinson Crusoe's," she said with a tiny smile.

"But nothing compares to the Donner party's…"

She fisted her hand and punched him in the upper arm. "They weren't castaways, you dope. And just so you know, if we have to resort to cannibalism by tomorrow, I've been told I'm very stringy."

He laughed and ran his fingertips down her soft, feminine arm. She watched him, tensing, but didn't pull away.

"There's not a stringy thing about you," he said. "You're absolutely perfect."

She shifted her gaze away, visibly nervous, and he suspected she, too, had been thinking about the fact that they were stranded here, alone, for the entire night.

After the loaded conversation they'd shared by the waterfall when she'd revealed so much of herself, he imagined she'd have preferred a chance to go to her stateroom, curl up in bed and lick her wounds. But she wasn't getting that chance.

He would have to tread carefully. The last thing he wanted was to make her feel any worse, or make her think he didn't understand. Or that he hadn't opened up his mind to the possibility that he'd been very, *very* wrong.

"Me make fire. Ugh. Strong like bull."

She snickered, the tension dying. "Yes, caveman, now come sit down and have some of this magnificent caviar. It may not be Beluga, but we'll just have to rough it tonight."

He groaned dramatically. "If we must."

Although they had the table and two chairs, he grabbed one of the sleeping bags and spread it out beside the crackling fire. The air was cooling as the sun fell farther toward the horizon. Here, on the eastern shore, they wouldn't be able to see it set. They could only watch as it disappeared behind the jungle of trees running down the middle of the island. And within minutes, the shadows of dusk spread across the beach and the softly blowing breeze began to carry the faintest hint of a chill.

They ate their spectacular picnic on the blanket, enjoying the caviar, as well as leftover jerk chicken from this afternoon's cookout, plus fruits and cheeses, spicy-sweet grilled plantains and even slices of coconut cream pie. There was still plenty of food left for a midnight snack and breakfast tomorrow, plus several bottles of water.

They'd be fine. Absolutely fine. Nothing bad could happen, and maybe something very good would come of this enforced proximity.

"Oh, crap, what is that?"

Hearing tension in her voice, Nate followed her stare toward the water. "What?"

But she didn't have to answer. A sharp, bright light rent the sky over the ocean. Probably miles away, but definitely powerful enough to pierce the darkness of the evening sky.

"It's heat lightning. That's all."

His words had no sooner left his mouth than a long, low rumble of thunder split the night.

"Perfect," Heather said. She drew closer to him. "Do you think the storm is headed this way?"

"Nah," he said, willing it to be true. "It's probably miles from here." Forcing a laugh, he added, "Serves everyone on the boat right. I hope they get rained out, too."

Her giggle was a little shrill, but she tried to keep

up the positive thinking. "Maybe they'll have to play charades for entertainment."

"Whew, we dodged a bullet on that one, Red."

Suddenly, the wind picked up. Hard, cool gusts came off the water, carrying sand, grit and salt spray right toward them. They were close to the water's edge, and he noticed how the normally soft, gentle waves were growing larger and rolling in closer together, hitting the shore with audible intensity. Each was capped with white foam, as whatever was happening at sea affected the surf.

"I think we're in trouble," Heather said, having to raise her voice above the sound of the surf and the wind.

Lightning flashed again, closer now, a magnificent display. A loud clap of thunder came right on its heels.

Shit. She was right. They weren't going to escape this. The storm was headed right toward them.

He immediately got to his feet, pulling her to hers. "We can't stay on the beach," he snapped. "The sand is wet. This is the last place we want to be in a lightning storm."

She nodded. Her lips moved, but no sound came out. Her eyes were wide, a little frightened, and he stroked her cheek to try to calm her down.

"We'll be fine. Grab the sleeping bags and follow me. We have to find a clearing where I can set up the tent."

She didn't ask questions. One thing he loved about Heather, she knew how to keep her head. Together, they grabbed what they needed and headed for the treeline, the wind buffeting them along. The rain hadn't started yet, but the lightning was closer than ever, the thunder rumbling right over their heads.

"What about here?" she called as soon as they were

under the canopy. "It'll give us more shelter than just the tent."

He shook his head and kept going, glad for the flashlight setting on his phone. "We can't risk being under a tree."

Again, she didn't argue. They went about fifteen yards into the jungle before they reached a spot flat and open enough for him to feel comfortable. "Hold the light for me while I set this tent up, would you? We'll be inside, safe and dry, in just a minute."

He hoped.

She did, aiming the beam of the phone light toward the ground as he quickly unfolded the tent. Thankfully, it was a pretty simple, pop-up style, easily big enough for the two of them. Nate got it spread out, slammed some supportive stakes into the ground, tied it off and then extended the poles. They were about five feet tall, strong and thick, and should be enough to keep the hopefully waterproof, nylon tent securely in place.

Thick plops of rain started to come down just as he finished. He grabbed the sleeping bags and tossed them inside.

"Come on."

Heather took a step toward him, but then froze. "Wait, Nathan, all our stuff is right by the water."

"Forget it, come on."

"But the surf might wash everything away. We might need food and water! What if the boat gets caught in the storm and can't get back here in the morning?"

She headed for the beach, but she only took two steps before another massive lightning bolt turned night to day, right over their heads. The lightning was accompanied by a massive crash of thunder that sounded as explosive as a cannon.

Nate yelled a warning, realizing Heather was standing under a huge tree, which was swaying wildly in the rough wind. He suddenly envisioned that tree coming down on her, or the lightning hitting her.

Panic filled him. Reacting purely on instinct, he ran right toward her, faster than he ever had on the field. Nate saw nothing but her terrified face, was focused on nothing but keeping her safe.

He dove, catching her around the waist, and rolled with her out from under the tree. Even as they bumped across the wet ground, he heard the sound of a limb snapping and caught the scent of electric fire. Not until they were several feet away, halfway under a bush, did he even take a breath. For a long moment, he just held her close, hugging her protectively under his body, both of them shaking and shuddering.

A quick glance out from under the bush confirmed his deepest fear. The tree had split in two. Half of it remained upright. The other half was lying in a tangled heap of limbs and branches. Right where Heather had been standing.

If he'd been a few seconds later, if his reflexes had been slower, she might have been badly injured. Or even killed.

He squeezed her tighter until she gasped, but even then he didn't let her go. He couldn't help it, couldn't let her out of his arms, not now when he'd realized in those few frantic seconds just how much she meant to him.

Not now that he knew he was madly in love with the woman.

Her words about how short and precarious life could

be had been lurking in the back of his mind. And when he'd been confronted by that awful possibility, all the self-protective instincts that had warned him not to let anybody get too close had disappeared. Nothing had mattered except Heather.

The brief glimmer of an instant when he'd envisioned life without her had reinforced the truth. If he wanted her, he had to trust her with every bit of himself—his mind, his body, his heart. He had to open himself up to all the emotion he'd told himself he didn't want. Had to let himself feel it and trust she would never betray it.

In that moment, he knew he did. He trusted her completely.

And he was never going to let her go.

THE STORM LASTED for a few hours, the rain coming down in a torrential tidal wave. The skies quaked and the never-ending bolts of lightning brightened even the inside of the tent.

But they were safe.

Curled up together on the sleeping bags, they focused on each other and not on what was happening outside. And, gradually, the wicked tropical storm began to die down. The lightning bolts became fewer, the thunder rumbled much farther in the distance, the gusty wind ceased its howl. The rain continued to fall, but with a little less ferocity, and the tent kept them snug and dry. Eventually, Heather even stopped shaking.

"You okay now?" Nate asked, apparently feeling her finally relax in his arms.

"Yes," she whispered, wishing she could see his face in the darkness, wanting the reassurance of that sexy smile. But his arms, his hot body, were a pretty good substitute, and when his mouth found hers in the darkness, she kissed him back, sighing in pleasure.

Definite pleasure. He moved his hands up and down her spine, dropping one to cup her ass, squeezing gently. Heather said nothing, merely slipping out of her skirt and swimsuit, and pulling his clothes off him. She pushed him onto his back and sat astride him, needing to feel a little more in control than she had earlier tonight.

He seemed to understand, letting her set the pace, the tone, everything. His hands on her hips, he led her to him, ready for her, as she'd known he would be. Just as she was ready.

Holding her breath, Heather lowered herself onto his rigid cock, taking him into her body. She sank all the way down in one slow motion, until he was fully sheathed within her, and stayed that way for a few long moments.

He reached for her face, brushing his thumb over her lips and murmuring, "I've never been more scared in my life than when I saw you under that tree."

"I know, I'm sorry," she replied, slowly beginning to rock on him, gentle thrusts that gave both pleasure and comfort.

It went on for a long while, the achingly sweet but equally sultry loving. Their bodies became coated with sweat, their hot breaths loud in the small tent. Heather forgot about everything going on outside, focusing only on the storm of emotion in her heart and the tsunami of desire in her body.

Eventually, he rolled her over and moved between her thighs, driving into her again and again. Heather arched up to meet every thrust. She wrapped her arms around his neck, bringing his mouth to hers, wanting not one inch of humid air between them. And when they both reached the highest peak, she whispered his name against his lips as they came.

Afterward, they slept for a while, naked and tangled together, hot bodies in the hot night.

When she awoke, she could hear only the softest patter of rain on the tent. She shifted out from under him, reached for the zipper on the end of the tent and drew it down.

"Storm's almost over," he murmured.

"Yes, seems so." She looked out at the pile of limbs fifteen feet away, where she had come so close to being crushed. She shivered, and Nate drew her close, kissing her brow.

"Do you think they're okay?" she whispered.

"I'm sure the captain outran the storm," he replied, knowing exactly what she meant. "They'll be fine. And so will we."

"Thanks to you."

He cleared his throat. "I don't just mean physically."

Heather lay back down with him, noting that she could again see his face. The storm clouds had mostly blown by, and enough moon and starlight sifted through the trees and the tent to enable her to make out his handsome features.

"I need to tell you something," he said.

She knew by his tone that whatever he wanted to say was important. "Okay."

"I've spent the last ten months clearing my name. And my head."

"Yes, it must have been awful."

"That's an understatement. The reporters were ruthless." He sighed. "Felicity is America's darling right now."

Heather managed to bite back her opinion of the *darling*. Calling that witch a darling was like calling Lizzie Borden America's sweetheart.

"The day I found out about the pregnancy, I thought I was prepared for what was headed my way. I wasn't. I didn't really have a clue how far the paparazzi were willing to go until I caught a photographer hiding in my house."

She gasped. "He broke in?"

"I think he was hoping I'd hit him so he could press charges, or at least talk me into not pressing charges of my own. But my dad was with me, and he kept me cool enough to call the cops and let them handle it."

She couldn't imagine that. His life as a popular athlete was public enough. Being cast as a villain in Felicity Monroe's personal Shakespearean tragedy had made him a target of crime and vitriol.

"They started stalking my old college girlfriend, who's now a married mom. They followed me everywhere. Went through my trash and reported that I'd thrown away a baby blanket, hand knit by Felicity, which was complete bullshit."

She remembered that headline. "She doesn't look like the knitting type."

"That's for sure," he said with a chuckle. "Anyway, I can only imagine how the press would have treated the 'mysterious redhead' who 'stole' me away from Miss MTV, which is how she would have spun it."

"I hate her." Able now to at least grasp what she might have been in for, Heather said, "Thank you for trying to protect me. I know that's why you ended things and stayed away."

"Yeah, it is, but that's not why I'm telling you this. What I want to say is, Felicity told me many times that she'd done it for love."

"What, cheated on you?"

He nodded.

She didn't quite understand. "So, she wanted to rub it in that she was in love with this other guy?"

He snorted. "No, she did it out of love for me."

"Oh, *that's* a unique approach."

"Manipulative, remember? She said she was using him. He was a music producer and she wanted his undivided attention. She also hoped that cheating with him would get *my* undivided attention, which she thought she was losing. She was so desperate to hold on to me, she had to make me jealous."

"Was that the truth?"

It took a while for him to answer. She wondered if he'd even evaluated that himself, what he'd been feeling before his relationship had so publicly imploded.

Finally, he said, "I guess it was. I was pretty infatuated with her at first—or, at least, the persona that she presented to me. I proposed quickly and was shocked when she said yes."

"Are you kidding? She knew an amazing thing when she saw it." She squeezed his hand. "Don't sell yourself short."

"I don't mean to. But she was the hottest thing on the air, dating movie stars and rap moguls."

"And you were the hottest thing on the field, sexier than any man has a right to be, and probably making tons of money."

"Yeah, the money definitely had something to do with it. As did notching her belt with somebody who'd never been linked to another celebrity before."

Linked to celebrity. Yes, she supposed star quarterbacks usually were. And nobody would ever mistake Heather for somebody famous.

But, she suddenly realized, she didn't care. Because unlike the Felicity types of the world, she really understood what love was. She was capable of loving someone enough to do just about anything to keep him from being hurt. The idea of doing something as awful as falsifying paternity and trying her lover in the court of public opinion was utterly abhorrent to her.

"But of all the things I went through, I think I resent her the most for twisting my mind around when it came to love and commitment. She made me believe that love was about manipulation, jealousy, cheating and dishonesty. I got this idea that it was all wrapped up together, that it was impossible to have one without all the rest."

Heather gasped, suddenly understanding why he'd brought this up. He was trying to explain to her why he could not love her, why he couldn't commit, not now, not in the future.

She blinked away tears, and said, "I understand. You really don't have to say anything more." Her faint sniffle might have clued him in to the fact that she was lying, but she hoped he'd believe it was because of the damp night air.

"Of course I have to say more," he said, suddenly sitting up. He drew her up, too, until they were face-to-face. The rain had finally stopped and the clouds had thinned even more. Through the unzipped flap, moonlight eased in, falling on their faces.

His expression was tender. Sweet. Loving. A look she hadn't imagined she'd ever see again.

"Heather, I was wrong. I was so totally wrong. You came so close to being hurt—or worse—and, well, all I could think of was what I'd do if I lost you again."

He lifted his hand to her face, touching her cheek, brushing his fingers through her hair. She kissed his palm, feeling her heart start to skid and tumble in her chest. Her pulse was tumbling, too, her blood rushing fast through her veins as she tried to grasp what he was saying, not quite daring to believe it.

"I remembered what you said about your parents, and how fleeting life can be." He leaned closer, brushing his lips across hers, adding, "And I realized that I was wrong. I do believe in love, Heather Hughes."

She closed her eyes, breathing deeply, slowly.

"I've thought of nothing but you for the past ten months. When I was in the throes of the lawsuit, in court, dodging reporters or on the field throwing interceptions, I just kept dreaming about you."

"Really?" she whispered.

"Really." He kissed her again, and this time she kissed him back, parting her lips to let their tongues gently touch and caress. They'd made love moments ago, but the sweet eroticism aroused her all over again. She wanted him, and she knew she could never have enough of this man.

When their mouths drew apart, he said one more thing. "I love you."

She nodded slowly, believing it with all her heart. How could she not believe him when she felt the same way?

"I love you, too, Nate."

He pulled her onto his lap, kissing her cheek, her jaw, her neck, repeating the words over and over. It was as if, having dammed his emotions up inside himself for so long, he wanted to make sure there was not a single doubt about his feelings.

She didn't doubt him. She never would again.

Her sweet, sexy, playful man was back. And she'd never been happier to see anyone in her entire life.

They fell back down on the sleeping bags, exchanging kiss after kiss, murmuring soft words of love, until something occurred to Heather, and she had to laugh.

"What?"

"I was just thinking about how funny it would be if everyone on that boat caught us right now."

He nuzzled her neck. "If those jackasses who work for my father saw you like this, I'd have to kill them." He moved lower, licking her breast. "You're mine."

His. Oh, yes, indeed she was. For as long as he wanted her.

And she already knew, in her heart, that he wanted her for a lifetime.

As she did him.

Epilogue

THE ISLAND WEDDING was everything they had dreamed it would be. Beautiful. Intimate. Private. Just two people in love saying their vows on the shores of a crystal blue sea, beneath swaying palm trees, to the beat of calypso drums.

Heather had never thought about getting married on a beach, but having seen how beautiful her mother and Jerry's ceremony had been the year before, she'd realized it was what she wanted, too.

Without the sea voyage and two dozen guests, however.

With Nate still very much in the spotlight, especially after his spectacular winning season, they'd wanted to try to sneak a private moment, in a private place, to exchange vows. Neither of them had wanted a public circus, and even though the Felicity scandal had blown over—her lover's wife had found out and caused a media sensation—they were still on the radar of some nosy paparazzi. Maybe the press was trying to figure out why on earth Nate had chosen her when he could have had an international pop star.

Heather didn't wonder. She and Nate shared a once-in-a-lifetime love. Having lived together in Miami for the past year, neither of them had a single doubt about spending the rest of their lives together.

"How are you feeling, Red?"

"Happier than I've ever been in my life," she said as they walked hand-in-hand down the sugar-white St. Lucian beach after they'd been pronounced husband and wife.

He lifted her hand and kissed her fingertips. "Me, too. And also relieved."

"Why?"

"I fully expected wedding crashers."

She grimaced. "Reporters?"

"No. The 'rents. I would have sworn your mom was going to sneak down here."

Laughing, she conceded, "I am sure she wanted to, but she understood. Just be prepared for our reception next week to be the social event of the season." Although Heather and Nate spent most of their time in Miami, they had bought a place in Albuquerque so they could be near family. They spent a lot of the football off-season there and would have a big celebration with friends and family when they got home to the States. "Besides, she's still feeling tremendously guilty about stranding us on that island last year."

"She shouldn't. That turned out to be the most important night of my life."

And Heather's.

Heather had long ago forgiven the prank. What was a little storm compared to finding out the man of her dreams truly loved her?

"Did you ever envision your mom as a business-woman?"

Laughing, Heather said, "No, but don't make fun. She's having the time of her life, and Santa Fe is crazy for her."

After moving to Florida last spring, Heather had opened a new gallery in South Beach, and Amy had taken over the one in New Mexico. The business might not be a huge success, since her mom was a sucker for a sob story, but Amy Hughes—now Watson—was certainly building her gallery's reputation as the place to go for eccentric, eclectic, joyful pieces.

She'd even changed the name. To Flibbertigibbet's.

How wonderful.

They continued to walk along the shore, kicking their feet in the surf as the sun dropped low in the sky. Beams of orange, yellow and red danced across the surface of the waves, as if the sky itself were putting on a light show just for them.

They talked about the future, about the past. About her father and his mother. About the children they would someday have.

Mostly, they talked about love. How much they felt it. How close they'd come to losing it. How very precious it was to them both.

And how they were never—ever—going to let it go.

* * * * *

Dear Reader,

Aloha! I'm so excited to be writing this letter to you for my first ever Harlequin Blaze book. Gee, I've been waiting for close to thirty years for this moment, and here it is. I'm so honored to be paired with Leslie Kelly, too!

Have you ever been to Hawaii? Ever flown first class? Or lived on the edge? You get to in *More Than a Fling*. I adore writing about places I've been and bringing them to life. The excitement. The passion. The vacation nuance. From the first moment Lana and Grant meet we can feel their attraction and chemistry. I'm so happy to be able to bring their story to you, and I hope you fall in love with them as much as I have.

Please visit me at my website, shanagray.com, to keep on top of all the exciting things coming up, and please sign up for my newsletter, too. I would be thrilled to hear from you and know what you think of my first ever Harlequin Blaze.

Enjoy and hang loose (a totally Hawaiian term)!

Mahalo,

Shana Gray

MORE THAN A FLING

Shana Gray

My mom was my champion. It didn't matter what I had going on, or if she approved or didn't, she was behind me a hundred percent. She was my first phone call for good and bad news. We lost Mom suddenly in December 2012, and I miss her terribly. After I got The Call from Kathleen Scheibling, Mom was the first person I thought of. This book is dedicated to her. How I wish she was here to share in my good news and excitement and that glass of champagne. Dad has become my new champion. At 92 he's stepping into the roll with gusto. xo

_1_

LANA WOKE WITH a start. The lights were dimmed and the plane was hushed. This was the last leg of her trip—Sydney behind her, Hawaii in time for breakfast. One flight seemed to roll into the next. Damn that international dateline. It always screwed her up.

Her wineglass and dinner dishes had been cleared away and someone had draped a blanket over her legs. First class sure had top-notch service. Too bad she didn't have someone to share it with. Lana sighed and rubbed her eyes. She had to pee, and a freshen up would be nice, too.

She felt her way through the darkened cabin to the lavatory—perfect timing for the plane to hit a pocket of turbulence. Lana lost her footing, didn't see the door open and catapulted headlong into the person coming out. Not just any person, but a mountain of a man. She reached out to steady herself, her fingers closing around some very impressive, muscled shoulders. Arms snaked around her like steel bands, holding her tighter than she'd ever been held before.

Lana gasped. He smelled so damn good, too. She

blinked and looked up—way up. This man was huge, built, broad, tanned, blond… Viking blond with brown eyes that reminded of her of chocolate syrup. Sticky, sweet, sinfully delightful. She swallowed when her heart tripped over itself, and she felt her panties growing moist. This is what she got for being celibate for so long.

He stared back at her, the right side of his mouth curved up in a smile.

Wanna join the Mile High Club, you sexy beast, you? Lana almost blurted the words and fought like hell to bite her tongue. Literally. Wild, spontaneous, sex with a stranger wasn't her game. She wasn't shy about sex, oh, no, but banging a dude within seconds of first laying eyes on him was…what? Wrong? Not exactly. Just not something she'd done before, and boy was he making her want to change that.

"Um, excuse me." She was locked in his gaze, let herself stay in its magnetic pull. She didn't fight the warm, deep arousal that swelled inside her, enjoying the heat that flushed through her body as his arms held her so safe. Oh, God yes, he was so solid.

Aw, shit. Nothing like being horny on this never-ending godforsaken, grueling flight with no chance to—

"My apologies."

Gawd help me! He's got an accent.

Lana loved the South African cadence, and his was just as thick and sweet as the desire sweeping through her.

"No, it was my fault. I wasn't paying attention."

"That little bump in the road was somewhat of a surprise as well, ya."

Keep talking.

"Uh, yes. Yes, it was." The words dried up in her mouth when he pivoted her into the small area between the lavatory doors. He held her firmly and a little too closely, but Lana wasn't going to argue. What were the odds in life a girl would be this close to such a fine specimen of a man? Nevah! She would enjoy every second of this close encounter. Oh, yes.

The plane lurched again, throwing her against him. Now breast to chest, hips to hips, thighs to thighs, Lana felt every nuance of him. She curled her arms around his neck and hung on as the jet bounced through the night sky. Mr. Viking didn't pull away—she could have sworn she felt his arms tighten a bit more around her.

Sweet.

The jet's path smoothed out, and Lana began to feel foolish in his arms. The right thing to do would be to step away. Step away from the man. Away from the gorgeous hunk of maleness that made her want to drag him into the lavatory behind them.

Lana opened her eyes. The sign on the lavatory door right in front of her caught her attention. *Vacant.* All she had to do was open said door and push Mr. Viking inside, inviting them both into the Mile High Club. She swung her gaze to him and her heart flipped. He was watching her with an intensity that made her tremble. Was he thinking the same thing?

Reluctantly Lana stepped from the captivating heat of his embrace. The lingering aura of his power didn't dwindle with the distance.

"Can I escort you to your seat?"

Oh, a gentleman, too.

"Well, actually… I need to…" Lana nodded to the lavatory door and nearly died when her cheeks heated.

He laughed and her knees wobbled. Good God, he was getting under her skin.

"Of course." His voice was low and he bowed his head before murmuring, "If you care to join me after, I'll order us a nightcap whilst you're engaged."

Whilst? He certainly was proper. Lana tipped her head back to gaze at him, knowing she couldn't say no. "Yes, please. That would be delightful."

Delightful? Holy shit, when had she become Ms. Formal? Lana fled into the lavatory before she could make a further ass of herself.

A few minutes later, Lana hurried back down the aisle. It wasn't hard to find him, as he stood for her.

"Please." He indicated the seat by the window, placing his hand on the small of her back to guide her.

His touch elicited a thrill of pleasure. "Thank you." Lana sat and curled a leg under herself, twisting in the seat to face him.

Soft light from the table surface between them illuminated them in a cocoon of intimacy. Excitement pooled in her belly and Lana decided then and there to throw caution to the wind and see where this may take her.

"So, tell me about yourself. What brings you to fly from Oz to Hawaii?" she asked.

"A short layover—business. I'm actually flying on to Vancouver next week."

"Really? I'm heading to Toronto, via Vancouver. Next week, as well." She paused. "Maybe we're on the same flight."

"Well then, what would be the odds of that?" His voice was so smooth and deep, she wanted to hear more.

"Crazy. I'll be staying for about ten days. Kind of a vacation before a business meeting next week."

"So you weren't on vacation Down Under?"

"No, business, as well. I'm exhausted and need a rest." She nearly scowled as she thought about the meeting with her boss next week. She had a lot to prepare for, and damn if she'd let it get in the way of her downtime on the Aloha Isles. She hoped getting the meeting prep out of the way early would let her chill for the rest of the time.

He accepted the drinks from the flight attendant, offering one to Lana. Their fingers touched and a bolt of lust shot up her arm and found its way to her core. She raised the glass and took a long pull. Aged Scotch. Its fiery heat seared a trail down her throat and rather than quelling her desire it magnified it. The lavatory idea was getting more and more appealing.

"Where are you staying?" he inquired.

That was the quandary. She had nowhere at the moment. Adding vacation time before her meeting in Hawaii next week had happened at the last minute—only happened at all because she'd been able to switch her flight without fees. "Well, actually, I have tonight, or tomorrow, or will it be yesterday?" Lana laughed. "And the next four at the Moana. Then back at the hotel next week for the meeting. In between…" She shrugged. "And you?"

"I have a house on the North Shore."

It took all of Lana's willpower to not choke on her drink. "Really? Is it on the beach?"

He smiled and nodded. "It's older and not very big. A grass shack."

"I'm sure." Lana smiled at him. "Do you get there often?"

"Not often enough. We usually keep this month clear and rent it the rest of the year."

"We?" Shit. Was he married or otherwise entangled? No way would she be the other woman.

His smile was captivating. "My brother. We try to visit when our schedules allow."

OMG, a brother? Is he as gorgeous as...? Then Lana realized—"You know what? I don't know your name."

He laughed. "I'm Grant Rankin. And you?"

"Lana. Lana Hunter."

Grant held out his hand. "Nice to meet you, Lana Hunter."

His fingers, warm and strong, curled around hers. He didn't let her go and they stayed like that for a minute. Did she just imagine it, or did he lean in to her ever so slightly, perhaps for a kiss?

Her eyelids fluttered and she licked her lips.

Grant's gaze dropped to her mouth. Oh, how she wanted him to kiss her. Yes, she absolutely did. Should she wait for him to make the move or do it herself?

"So then—" the sultry tone in his voice matched the smoldering heat in his gaze "—I can offer you a room in the house if you like."

"Really?" A beach house in Hawaii with a hot dude? *Twist my arm.* But then Lana's conscience screamed at her. *You don't know him. He could be a serial killer.* She sat back a little and sipped, thinking frantically. Could she really accept this invite? She'd never considered anything like this before, and she was flustered. "That's very generous of you. I don't know what to say."

He smiled and put his glass down, letting go of her

hand. "Please, excuse me. It was a bit forward to suggest you stay with me."

"It's not that, just that, well—"

Grant placed his hand over hers again and tingles rippled across her flesh. "Just know that the offer stands."

What happened to the girl of moments ago throwing caution to the wind? Had she just lost an opportunity? She cast around for something else to talk about.

"You said you had a brother?" Dared she ask more? Yep. "No significant, ah…other?"

He raised his eyebrows, as if in surprise at her question, then shook his head.

"How about you? Any romantic connections?"

"No. No time and too much trouble."

"Trouble? How's that?"

Lana sighed, not really wanting to delve into it. But he'd responded to her questions, so she gave the bare minimum answer. No point going into all the gory details.

"I'm busy trying to get my career established. Relationships conflict with the travel I have to do." She waved her hand indicating the plane. "The perks are nice, though. First class is awesome. It's hard to meet new people and I abhor office romances, since most of them end with cheating and lying."

He laughed. "Very insightful. You've had an offensive experience with office romance?"

"Good God, no, but I've seen it and the wake of destruction it causes. I've had a few sketchy times with men that can't appreciate my career path. Now I like to keep my personal and professional life separate." She looked him squarely in the eye, curious what his reaction would be.

The flight attendant broke the moment by setting down a delicious-looking cheese tray for them. After she strolled off, Grant still had his fingers interlaced with hers. It was only a tad awkward to nosh and drink, but the touch of him was too new and exciting, and she wasn't ready to let him go just yet.

A few moments later, Grant reached into his shirt pocket and pulled a leather case out. He opened it with his thumb and retrieved a card, placing it on the table.

Lana glanced down.

Grant Rankin
President & CEO
Rankin & Lean Industries

"Take it and call any time."

Lana looked at him. Had she really only met him a few hours ago? It seemed as though she was with someone she'd known forever. She had to remind herself they'd just met and she didn't know him from Adam.

"Thank you."

He smiled at her and she returned it, loving the way she warmed under his gaze.

"Do you have a card?"

"Ah, yes. But, it's in my luggage. What do you do for business?"

He shrugged. "Nothing special. Enough to pay the bills and keep things exciting. Imports, acquisitions. I'm trying to grow my present business a little."

"Oh, really. Maybe we could talk about it sometime. I might be able to help with that."

He smiled and her belly tumbled over itself. Lana barely heard his reply and nodded dumbly, focusing on

FREE Merchandise is 'in the Cards' for you!

Dear Reader,

We're giving away FREE MERCHANDISE!

Seriously, we'd like to reward you for reading this novel by giving you **FREE MERCHANDISE** worth over **$20**. And no purchase is necessary!

You see the Jack of Hearts sticker above? Paste that sticker in the box on the Free Merchandise Voucher inside. Return the Voucher promptly…and we'll send you valuable Free Merchandise!

Thanks again for reading one of our novels—and enjoy your Free Merchandise with our compliments!

Pam Powers

Pam Powers

P.S. Look inside to see what Free Merchandise is **"in the cards"** for you!

W

e'd like to send you two free books like the one you are enjoying now. Your two books have a combined price of over $10, but they are yours to keep absolutely FREE! We'll even send you 2 wonderful surprise gifts. You can't lose!

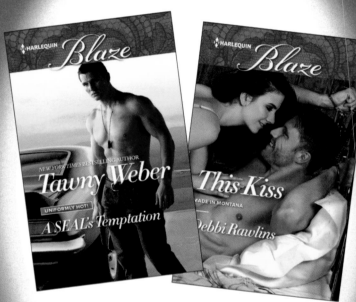

REMEMBER: Your Free Merchandise, consisting of **2 Free Books** and **2 Free Gifts**, is worth over $20.00! No purchase is necessary, so please send for your Free Merchandise today.

Get TWO FREE GIFTS!

We'll also send you two wonderful FREE GIFTS (worth about $10), in addition to your 2 Free books!

Visit us at:
www.ReaderService.com

Leslie Kelly
Shana Gray

———

A Taste of Paradise

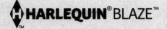
HARLEQUIN® BLAZE™

If you purchased this book without a cover you should be aware that this book is stolen property. It was reported as "unsold and destroyed" to the publisher, and neither the author nor the publisher has received any payment for this "stripped book."

ISBN-13: 978-0-373-79876-6

A Taste of Paradise

Copyright © 2015 by Harlequin Books S.A.

The publisher acknowledges the copyright holders of the individual works as follows:

Addicted to You

Copyright © 2015 by Leslie Kelly

More Than a Fling

Copyright © 2015 by Janine Whalley

All rights reserved. Except for use in any review, the reproduction or utilization of this work in whole or in part in any form by any electronic, mechanical or other means, now known or hereinafter invented, including xerography, photocopying and recording, or in any information storage or retrieval system, is forbidden without the written permission of the publisher, Harlequin Enterprises Limited, 225 Duncan Mill Road, Don Mills, Ontario M3B 3K9, Canada.

This is a work of fiction. Names, characters, places and incidents are either the product of the author's imagination or are used fictitiously, and any resemblance to actual persons, living or dead, business establishments, events or locales is entirely coincidental.

This edition published by arrangement with Harlequin Books S.A.

For questions and comments about the quality of this book, please contact us at CustomerService@Harlequin.com.

® and TM are trademarks of Harlequin Enterprises Limited or its corporate affiliates. Trademarks indicated with ® are registered in the United States Patent and Trademark Office, the Canadian Intellectual Property Office and in other countries.

Recycling programs for this product may not exist in your area.

Printed in U.S.A.

HARLEQUIN®
www.Harlequin.com

YOUR FREE MERCHANDISE INCLUDES...
2 FREE Books **AND** 2 FREE Mystery Gifts

► Detach card and mail today. No stamp needed. ►

© 2015 HARLEQUIN ENTERPRISES LIMITED ● and ™ are trademarks owned and used by the trademark owner and/or its licensee. Printed in the U.S.A.

FREE MERCHANDISE VOUCHER

2 FREE BOOKS and **2 FREE GIFTS**

Please send my Free Merchandise, consisting of **2 Free Books** and **2 Free Mystery Gifts**. I understand that I am under no obligation to buy anything, as explained on the back of this card.

150/350 HDL GJAT

Please Print

FIRST NAME

LAST NAME

ADDRESS

APT.#   CITY

STATE/PROV.   ZIP/POSTAL CODE

Offer limited to one per household and not applicable to series that subscriber is currently receiving.
Your Privacy—The Reader Service is committed to protecting your privacy. Our Privacy Policy is available online at www.ReaderService.com or upon request from the Reader Service. We make a portion of our mailing list available to reputable third parties that offer products we believe may interest you. If you prefer that we not exchange your name with third parties, or if you wish to clarify or modify your communication preferences, please visit us at www.ReaderService.com/consumerschoice or write to us at Reader Service Preference Service, P.O. Box 9062, Buffalo, NY 14269. Include your complete name and address.

NO PURCHASE NECESSARY!

B-N15-FM15

READER SERVICE—Here's how it works:

Accepting your 2 free Harlequin® Blaze® books and 2 free gifts (gifts valued at approximately $10.00) places you under no obligation to buy anything. You may keep the books and gifts and return the shipping statement marked "cancel." If you do not cancel, about a month later we'll send you 4 additional books and bill you just $4.74 each in the U.S. or $5.21 each in Canada. That is a savings of at least 14% off the cover price. It's quite a bargain! Shipping and handling is just 50¢ per book in the U.S. and 75¢ per book in Canada.* You may cancel at any time, but if you choose to continue, every month we'll send you 4 more books, which you may either purchase at the discount price or return to us and cancel your subscription. *Terms and prices subject to change without notice. Prices do not include applicable taxes. Sales tax applicable in N.Y. Canadian residents will be charged applicable taxes. Offer not valid in Quebec. Books received may not be as shown. All orders subject to approval. Credit or debit balances in a customer's account(s) may be offset by any other outstanding balance owed by or to the customer. Please allow 4 to 6 weeks for delivery. Offer available while quantities last.

◄ If offer card is missing write to: Reader Service, P.O. Box 1867, Buffalo, NY 14240-1867 or visit www.ReaderService.com ◄

BUSINESS REPLY MAIL
FIRST-CLASS MAIL   PERMIT NO. 717   BUFFALO, NY

POSTAGE WILL BE PAID BY ADDRESSEE

READER SERVICE
PO BOX 1867
BUFFALO NY 14240-9952

NO POSTAGE
NECESSARY
IF MAILED
IN THE
UNITED STATES

his kissable lips. This man was distracting her in such a sweet way. The end of this grueling trip was definitely looking up.

A short while later, Grant excused himself and wandered back to the lavatory. It was now or never. Lana dashed back to her seat and fished for her purse. She rummaged through it, looking for the condom she knew was in there somewhere. Lana found it tucked between sanitary napkins and pushed it into her pocket. As she made her way up the aisle, the cabin was dark, the quiet broken only by the hum of the engines as the plane flew north.

GRANT WASHED HIS hands and looked in the mirror. He was getting sick of these overnight flights. In fact, of flying in general. But the expansion of his business demanded it. On a positive note, it allowed him to meet a variety of people. He smiled, thinking of Lana. What a treat she was. Vibrant, and bubbly, and he was pretty sure she had no idea her sex appeal was so strong. Her ambition and seemingly carefree attitude was catching, and her smoldering allure reached right inside him and hit him hard.

He'd surprised himself by inviting her back to his house. Normally he was very cautious with women, keeping them at arm's length until he was sure about their intentions. Which meant there hadn't been many women coming to his home since his divorce. He thinned his lips thinking of that debacle. Thankfully he'd been wise enough with his business, investments and prenup that she'd only been able to get her hands on just over a quarter of his net worth. Fuck. Losing the assets he'd worked so hard for still burned his ass, but sometimes you had to pay to get rid of poison.

Grant was splashing water on his face when he heard a soft knock at the door. Grabbing a towel he wiped his face and slid the lock aside. In the blink of an eye the door was open, closed, locked and Lana had her arms wrapped around his neck and her mouth on his.

"What?" He couldn't have been more shocked.

She lifted her lips from his and laughed, a deep, husky sound that sent shivers down his spine and made his balls tighten. This woman was full of surprises.

As she tipped her head sideways and smiled, he ached to kiss her glistening lips again.

"So, are you a member of the Mile High Club?" Her seductive tone mesmerized him.

"No. Are you?"

She shook her head and tipped her face up, her eyes drifting closed, and in that moment Grant thought she was the most beautiful woman he'd ever seen. Pale skin, thick dark hair straight as a die hanging to her shoulders, eyes he wished she would open. He wanted to see her passion in those violet depths.

"Then I think we should rectify that," Grant whispered. He felt her tremble, and the flush that bloomed over her cheeks was enchanting. She opened her eyes and his breath caught. "What do you say, gorgeous?"

She raised her hand and he looked at what she had in her fingers. He grinned and plucked the package from them. Grant guided her to sit on the sink and leaned toward her. A soft sigh escaped her when he pressed his lips to the column of her neck, the quickening throb of her pulse encouraging him.

He circled her waist, sliding his hands up her back,

pressing her to him. The fullness of her breasts against his chest made him want to rip that top off. With one hand at the back of her neck, he pushed his fingers into the silky thickness of her hair and held her head steady.

Nibbling along her jawbone until he found her mouth, Grant ran his tongue over her lips. She opened for him and he didn't wait, sealing his mouth on hers, his cock straining in his pants. Lana wrapped her legs around his hips, and he pushed into her heat, their clothing a frustrating barrier. He was about to reach down when she beat him to it.

Her hands, frantic on his belt and zipper, freed him quickly. He groaned when she curled her fingers around his cock and slid them along the shaft, giving a squeeze at the tip. Reaching for her, he grasped her thigh and slid his hands up to cradle her ass, then under her skirt. He slid his fingers under her panties along her slick, swollen folds. She moaned into his mouth and Grant deepened their kiss, sucking on her tongue while he thrust his finger into her.

With her hands on his cock and his fingers inside her, Grant knew it wouldn't be long before they both came. The risk of discovery, being in a public place, only heightened his arousal. A quickie at 40,000 feet was a first for him and he hoped wouldn't be the last with her.

He lifted his head and Lana opened her eyes. They gazed at each other for the briefest moment until they turned their attention to the package he ripped open. She was nodding but not saying anything, and Grant quickly sheathed himself.

"Yes or no?" Grant looked deep into her eyes to make sure this was what she really wanted. "There'll be no going back in a few seconds."

"Wasn't it me that got this ball rolling?" She smiled and raised her knees, giving him more access. "If I didn't want this, I wouldn't be here."

Grant held his cock and bumped gently against her opening, liking how her eyes fluttered shut and she licked her lips. Her hands rested over his on her thighs and she pulled him toward her. He needed no other invitation, with no time to woo or seduce her here in the confines of an airplane bathroom—that would come later, he would make sure of it—Grant drove deep into her waiting heat.

He felt her hand between them, and he fucked her with deep pulsing thrusts while she swirled her fingers on her clit. She tightened around him and sucked in a breath. Instinctively he knew she was going to come so he held off his own release. Her body tensed and bucked against him. Grant closed his arms around her to hold her tight, not wanting her to hurt herself in the confines of the lavatory. Trying to keep the noise to a minimum, Grant covered her mouth with his and kissed her deeply. She cried into him as her orgasm overcame her. One final, deep thrust and Grant released into her. His legs spread wide, he braced his feet against the wall and pressed into her with an orgasm that nearly turned him inside out.

Lana's head fell back against the mirror. Grant got his feet back under him and disposed of the condom. Seeing Lana sprawled as she was on the counter with her knees spread wide, her glistening pussy still swollen and pink, eyes closed, chest rising and falling as she caught her breath, Grant thought he'd never seen anything more damn sexy in his entire life. He wanted her again. But not here. He would make love to her next time, not just have a quick fuck. He wanted more. To get to know her. Discover her. Explore her.

"Come on, gorgeous, we've probably been in here long enough, ya."

Lana sat up with a sigh, blinking as if she didn't know where she was. Grant lifted her down and fixed her skirt, then placed a gentle kiss on her lips.

"Yes, you're right," she murmured.

"Here." Grant handed her a damp towel and she wiped her brow.

She glanced up at him with a smile that worked its way into his heart. Yes, he definitely was going to get to know her better.

"We've both been initiated. Not everyone can say they're a member of the Mile High Club." She laughed and stood on her toes to kiss his cheek. "Now, can we get back to our seats without everyone guessing what happened in here?"

2

LANA STOOD ON the balcony overlooking water. It was a spectacular view but something was missing. She thumbed the business card in her hand and dared to think of calling Grant.

After their tryst in the bathroom, they'd talked the rest of the flight, laughing softly in the hushed and sleeping cabin and sharing breakfast as they flew into the rising sun. She was intrigued by him and wished they could have spent more time together. The closer they flew to their destination the more upset Lana felt. Not over the fact they'd had frantic sex in the lavatory—she didn't regret that for a minute and she hoped he didn't, either. It was leaving him once they arrived in Honolulu that had her all twisted up inside. When they'd parted at the airport, Lana was a hot mess of emotion, which she carefully kept concealed from Grant.

He'd taken her into his arms, held her tight and kissed her goodbye. The feel of his lips on hers still lingered, as did the tenderness between her thighs. She touched her fingers to her mouth now, reliving the moment. It had started out gentle and friendly, but in a blink of an eye he had deepened the kiss, demanding she give more to him—and she did. No words had been spoken as raw emotion ripped them both open there on the sidewalk outside the arrival terminal.

Lana had clung to him, not wanting to let him go. When he fisted her hair as if he didn't want to let go either, she'd melted.

He'd offered her a lift in his chauffeur-driven vehicle. She was tempted, God how she was tempted. But she didn't accept. After too many heartbreaks, she'd decided men were not worth the trouble of a full-blown relationship. A fling in an airplane, fine. She was thankful to Grant for breaking her sexual dry spell, getting her back in the saddle, so to speak. But this couldn't be anything more. So she'd taken a taxi. He'd accepted her decision and didn't press her, but she did see a flash of disappointment in his eyes.

Grant had seen her into the cab and paid the driver before she could argue about it. He stood on the curb, a pink lei around his neck, long blond hair lifting in the sweetly scented breeze with his hand raised in farewell. Would their paths ever cross again? He'd grown smaller as they drew farther apart and she almost had the cabbie stop when the welling sense of panic seemed as if it might suffocate her.

Now she wished she had stopped him so she could have raced right back into Grant's arms.

A sob caught in her throat. *What the hell is the matter with me?* He was just a man she'd met on a plane and had a fling with before they both moved on. A lovely distraction, this interlude with a gorgeous man. Lana studied the card. She itched to call him. He told her to call her any time, but maybe that was just in the heat of the moment. Had he meant it? Could she call him?

Everything in her screamed *yes*. Was there anything wrong with a holiday fling? Technically, she wasn't on holiday, she was on a business trip with an extended layover in Hawaii she was calling a vacation. Next week she had to meet her tetchy boss on his own layover. He would be headed to Australia with information she needed to provide. Lots of work was in front of her, so maybe it was for the best. She needed to focus on her job. Right? After all, she was climbing that corporate ladder and was only a quarter of the way up. Then again, the meeting was a week away. She had time to enjoy a few days of rest in paradise.

Lana stayed on the balcony, staring out over endless waves. The sun sank below the horizon into a spectacular sunset. Was Grant thinking about her?

She gripped the balcony railing, needing to pull herself out of this. It was stupid. Why should she be so upset about a man she'd met, banged and left? That was all it was. A sweet, no-strings tryst between two strangers. Yet she was overcome with a sense of loss. *I still can't believe I did that, by the way.* So the chances of him being *the one* was remote, indeed. The tear that dripped down her cheek surprised the hell out of her and she wiped it away. *Snap out of it, already. No man is worth the emotional mess.* She turned her back on the glorious sunset and stepped into her room, tossed the business card on the table beside her phone and did her best to forget about both.

GRANT POURED HIMSELF a glass of wine. He only had a couple of Bellingham locked in the wine cooler, saving them for a special day, but decided he needed the superb taste to quell the lingering scent and exquisite taste on his tongue of Lana. Annoyed, disappointed, horny and mad as hell at himself for letting Lana go so easily, he yanked the chair around to the railing but didn't sit. He hadn't gone all caveman and thrown her over his shoulder, but it had taken all his control not to.

Grant raised the glass to his nose and inhaled the fragrance. A good vintage. This trip would be chaotic, with the major meeting next week falling in between the vineyard negotiations. He wanted the ancient earth lands in South Africa something fierce. Grant swirled the glass to release the bouquet of the wine and then sipped. Delicious.

Just like Lana. She had been a delight to talk to on the plane. Each minute they were together she'd enchanted him more. Not only did she have a sultry allure that had effectively snagged him by the balls, she was damn smart. A refreshing change. And as far as he could tell, she didn't know who he was, which was even more intriguing. They'd talked nonstop on the long flight and he felt as if he'd known her for years. Yet, he sensed she'd been holding back. Which made him curious about her. The fact she was vehement about office flings made him cautious—not that they were coworkers. But they were both flying in for meetings and Grant thought he recognized her description of her boss. Maybe it was a coincidence, but…

Still, he couldn't discuss it with her due to the level of secrecy needed for this venture.

He was still shocked that she'd come to him in the bathroom. It turned him on now to think about it. Shit, it was one of the sexiest things he'd ever experienced.

The fact that it was all her doing was even more exciting and made him wonder what else was up her sleeve.

Grant raised his glass and sipped the wine, trying to appreciate it. He watched the sky darken, revealing an explosion of stars. His surroundings faded as he relived the last kiss they'd shared at the airport. She certainly had gotten under his skin very quickly. He even missed the sound of her voice, the scent of spicy citrus coming from her dark hair, which had been like pure silk between his fingers.

She was different, independent and not clingy. She seemed determined to do her own thing. He wanted Lana. And what he wanted, he usually got. Or took. Why hadn't he persuaded her to come with him?

Grant tossed back the last of the wine and slammed the goblet onto the antique koa table. The stem snapped off and he frowned. Abandoning the broken crystal, Grant rested his palms on the wood railing, an idea forming. In business he made quick decisions, able to see the pros and cons almost immediately. This decision took a bit more thought. He had to do it right. Or he'd wind up right where he was now.

Alone. Frustrated.

Why couldn't he get her out of his head? Perhaps the fact that she hadn't come with him was what set her apart. And, he had to admit, their sexual frenzy a mile high had him wanting more of her.

"Right, then." His mind made up, he left the lanai and grabbed the keys to the vintage Ferrari.

Grant smiled when the roar of the engine filled the night air when he turned the key. He loved his cars. Right up there next to wine and, of course, women. He backed out of the garage, where he housed his babies, past his loaded off-road Jeep and the 1965 Porsche Speedster. The rest of his collection was at home on the Cape. Maybe if what he had planned tonight worked out, the Jeep would be in business tomorrow. Wheeling around he stepped on the gas. The tires spit the crushed shells from the driveway when he peeled out onto Ke Nui Road.

The highway was clear and he made good time to Waikiki. Coming to a screeching halt at the Moana, he climbed from the sports car and tossed the keys to the valet, palming him a hundred dollar bill.

"I'll be right back. Leave her here, please."

"Yes, sir."

In the lobby he looked around, appreciating the graciousness of the old hotel. It was beautiful and airy, hinting at the grandeur of days past. At the desk he greeted the clerk, sliding another bill across the counter.

"Good evening. Lana Hunter's room, please."

"Good evening, sir, thank you." The clerk expertly slipped the bill under some papers and inquired, "Are you expected?"

"No, I'm surprising her."

"Ah, very nice. However, I'm sorry, but I can't provide that information."

Even with the encouragement of money, this hotel was rigid. Another thing he appreciated. "Please ring her, then."

"Right away." The clerk picked up the phone. "Who may I say is asking?"

"Please tell…ask her to come down. If you don't mind, tell her she has a message to pick up."

The clerk smiled and spoke into the phone, then hung it up. "She said she would be down shortly."

"Thank you."

Grant settled into a chair facing the elevators, resting an ankle on one knee. It wasn't often he became excited about anything anymore and this unfamiliar feeling was quite welcome.

Ten minutes later, she stepped off the elevator. Damn if his heart didn't lurch just a little bit at the sight of her. The white shorts and cherry-colored tank top showed off her flawless skin, warmed from the sun. The sudden urge to lay her down and smooth cream over her body nearly choked him. Her breasts bounced under the top, evidence she was braless. He wanted to cup them in his palms and brush his fingers over her nipples, encouraging them to rise up. He hadn't given her breasts the attention they deserved earlier and he was anxious to see her fully naked.

Mesmerized by her, he was floored when her nipples did harden as if she knew he was watching her. Which had his cock sitting up and taking immediate notice. She seemed oblivious to the stir she caused as she strode through the lobby, a splash of vivid color in the grand atrium. The twinge in his groin made Grant bite back a groan. He fisted his hands on the armrests to keep them still and held his breath as she approached.

Grant rose and stepped toward her. The surprise on her face delighted him.

"Grant! What are you doing here?"

"I've come for you."

"Come for me? I don't understand."

"I'd like you to come back to my house with me." He didn't say *want*, that was too strong, almost an order.

He watched her. She was considering it. Would she hesitate? He stepped forward and took her elbow, about to encourage her a little more strongly to come. Her next words rushed like fire through his blood, straight to his cock.

"I'd love to. Give me a moment, there's a message for me."

"There's no message. I had the clerk tell you that to get you to come down."

She smiled. "I see. But I should get some—"

Grant put his arm around her shoulder, liking how she leaned into him, and turned her to head out the door. "We can get anything you need later. Now that I have you, I'm not letting you go again."

LANA COULDN'T BELIEVE this was happening to her. She was in a Ferrari, red like Magnum PI's, driving up the coast of Oahu to this hot dude's beach house. Thankfully she'd grabbed her purse on the way down for her so-called message. Other than what was in there, like lip gloss, a bit of emergency money and her room key, she didn't really need anything. She ignored the flash of alarm when she remembered she'd left her cell phone behind. She didn't need it right now, anyway.

The warm Hawaiian night caressed her skin and the wind blew through her hair. She let out an excited whoop as they ripped around a tight turn. At Grant's laugh, she looked over at him. He'd pulled his long hair back into a ponytail, which she thought was funny since hers was a wild riot around her head. His big hands gripped the wheel, and she knew deep inside that those hands would be on her tonight. A shiver rippled through her as arousal rose.

Lana let her thoughts run away, loving where they took her. In his house, in his bed, in his arms. His lips on hers, his hands on her body, her returning the favor. Him inside her, deep, hard, big, demanding. Lana closed her eyes and embraced the heat flaring in her pussy. So much for her sexual dry spell. She laughed out loud, and the wind whipped it away. Hell, after the year she'd had, didn't she deserve a little fun?

He seemed to be the right guy to have fun with. He had to be in his early thirties. Accomplished. Financially secure, clearly. Why wasn't he taken? Was there something wrong with him? He'd said he wasn't attached. She had to believe him. If he was, then she wouldn't be here with him. All she would allow this to be was a holiday affair. A wonderful fling with a heart-stopping man.

Pushing her hair out of her eyes, Lana glanced at Grant again, taking in his profile. His nose had a bit of a bump—broken before?—and his brows furrowed as he concentrated on the road. Her gaze lingered on his perfectly kissable lips, making her heart beat a little faster. Their kisses and touches had been far too frantic on the plane. Yes, this night would be wonderful. No strings, no pleas for a future, just two people enjoying each other.

Grant took her hand with one of his, brushing his thumb over the tender skin of her wrist. She moaned softly, sure he wouldn't hear it over the wind rushing around them. She was a ball of excited nerves.

A few minutes later he released her hand and geared the car down, taking a sharp turn onto a dark laneway. Trees hung over them and the sweet scent of frangipani filled the air.

"Almost there."

"I was beginning to wonder." Lana peered through

the bushes at the lights flickering through the foliage. They rounded an ancient banyan tree and she gasped. "This isn't a little old grass shack. Holy shit."

Grant burst out laughing and pulled up to the front entrance. "Stay there."

Lana waited for him to come around and open the car door. She took the hand he offered and was surprised when he pulled her into his arms and kissed her.

It wasn't a soft and gentle one. No sir, it picked up right where they left off at the airport. Lana moaned into his mouth, unable to contain her sexual need. Not wanting to. She opened for him when his tongue probed for hers.

The thin fabric of her top allowed the heat of his body to seep into her, spreading like a lava flow through her veins. Grant slipped his hands under her top, his fingers insistent and urgent on her skin, firing an explosive reaction down every nerve in her body. She lit up like a sparkler.

Curling her arms around his neck she bowed her back, wanting—needing—to get closer to him. Surface touch wasn't enough. She wanted him inside her.

Her lungs cried for air but pulling away from him would break the spell. She didn't want to breathe, she wanted to die right here in his arms. Under his kiss.

He pulled his mouth from her, his breathing as ragged as hers. Raising his eyebrows, he tilted his head toward the house. "Shall we go inside?"

She nodded like a bobble-head doll, unable to form cohesive thought. He'd knocked her world off its axis since the moment they met, what, less than twenty-four hours ago?

He swept her into his arms and carried her up the

wide coral slab steps, beneath the soft, artfully placed lights that gave a cozy glow to the entrance of the house. Lana tucked her face into his neck and breathed him in. His scent was exhilarating and reached right inside to clamp around her heart.

This was not love. Lana didn't believe in love at first sight anyway. It was purely lust. She was a big girl and being here with him was her decision. Getting lei'd Hawaiian style was just what she needed. Wanted. Her heart was too damaged to let its barricade down. Keys jangled as he unlocked the grand, beveled-glass front door. Pushing it aside he carried her over the threshold.

Lana glanced over her shoulder at the room before them. She gasped at the large, wide-open space with high wooden ceilings and shining floors. The furniture was exquisite and thick colorful area rugs were scattered about.

Floor-to-ceiling windows ran around three exterior walls and she could only guess at the spectacular view beyond. *Will I be here in the morning to see it?* The moon sparkled a glittering path across the surface of the waves toward them.

"Oh my God. This is amazing." Still in his arms, Lana looked up into his eyes. "This is definitely no grass shack."

He smiled at her and pressed a kiss to her lips. "It *is* old, and it was little until we renovated and added a few rooms."

"You're a tease." She murmured next to his lips, "So, are all the rooms as fabulous as this one?"

"Any particular one you're referring to?" His tone made her heart flip over and her belly flutter.

"Maybe." Lana pressed her lips to the base of his

neck, where the throbbing of his veins matched the pulsing of the blood through hers.

"Or we could go down to the cabana above the beach."

Lana didn't hesitate. "Yes, I'd like that."

He set her down. "You'll love it there. But first, let's get some wine. Wait here, I'll be right back."

While he was gone she wandered through the wide opening and out on to the deck. The windowless wall spanned the width of the room, floor to ceiling. It was glorious. Lana tilted her face upward and closed her eyes, loving the sultry feel of the breeze over her skin. She inhaled deeply. The night was still very warm and the scent of tropical flowers drifted on the gentle wind. It hadn't taken her long to fall in love with Hawaii, for more than one reason.

And she heard the main reason coming back.

He rested one hand on the curve of her neck, the other on her hip, and squeezed gently. "Shall we? Take your sandals off."

Lana nodded, slipped off her shoes and followed him outside, across a wide, magnificent deck and along a stone path beneath foliage and flowers aglow with unseen lights. It was so beautiful it took her breath away. They moved deeper into the tunnel of tropical branches. The sound of waves grew and then her toes sank into warm, powdery sand.

"Oh, this feels like heaven." Lana sighed.

"Do you want to swim?"

"It sounds rough. Is it safe to swim here?"

"Just off the beach is one of the few pools built centuries ago by an ancient Hawaiian king to keep his turtles handy for when he fancied a feast."

"That's horrible!"

"It's nothing to be alarmed about, it's how things were. That was long ago and now we use it for swimming."

Lana thought about it for a moment before answering, "I would, except I didn't bring a bathing suit."

Grant's soft chuckle reached her through the dark and she blushed. Bathing suit, indeed. If their antics earlier were any indication, she wouldn't be needing one.

A light flared off to the left. Grant had lit a torch, which cast a flickering circle of light on the sand and lapping waves. He walked out of the glow into the dark, and another torch blazed about twenty feet away. She could now see the gazebo perched above them at the edge of the merging torchlight.

A glorious structure. It stood on an outcrop of rock or coral, overlooking the sea. All kinds of tropical foliage skirted the cabana.

"How do you get up to there?" Lana asked as she scanned for a way up the slope.

"I'll show you."

Grant came to her side and tucked her arm through his. Heat flushed through her and her breasts tingled. She felt her nipples against the fabric of her top, reminding her she wasn't wearing a bra. *Good planning, chickie.* The feel of his flesh on hers was just as warm and sultry as the breeze blowing around them. She trembled for this man as she followed him to the cabana.

The gazebo was bigger than she'd expected. Grant unlocked and pushed back the wood shutters, opened gauzy draperies and tied them back with carefully knotted rope. Palms swayed like sentinels beside the lovely peaked roof. She was dying to see into the darkened interior.

"Come." He ushered her inside. "I forgot to bring the wine down with us, but I believe we have the fixings for a mai tai in the bar if you prefer."

"Perfect." Lana smiled at him and then looked around. "I've never seen anything like this. It's so beautiful."

"I'm glad you like it. Sit and I'll turn on some lights."

She settled on a wide chaise, wanting to tell him *not too many lights*. He must have read her mind, for moments later lights the size of rice grains twinkled to life in the beamed ceiling and around the columns supporting the intricately carved wooden roof. A fan rotated lazily, making the lights on the filigreed cord flutter and sparkle. She heard the clink of bottles and lay back on the chair.

"I'm overwhelmed. I've never, ever seen anything so breathtaking."

Grant placed the glasses on the rattan table by the chaise. She turned to meet his gaze.

"Neither have I." His low, husky voice held the promise of what was to come. Goose bumps rippled along her skin. God, he wasn't even touching her and he turned her on. Lana breathed steadily, trying hard not to anticipate what would happen when he actually did lay his hands on her.

His voice. His dangerous appeal. His amazing body. His insistence…his power. All of it so alluring and compelling.

She sucked in a breath and held it for a minute, hoping to slow her racing heart. She knew it was excitement and arousal all rolled up into churning passion and not a heart attack. Letting her breath out slowly, not wanting to look like a gasping fish, she kept her gaze fixed on his.

Her belly did a sweet little tumble. Oh Lord, he was a piece of candy she wanted to suck on. She didn't have to wonder how experienced he was, he oozed it. Had showed her quickly, ecstatically on the plane earlier. Tonight she wanted him slow and sensual.

Grant sat at the end of the chaise, still and calm, yet everything around him whirled and rushed in crazy chaos. Or was it just her? Everything was out of focus except him. What was he thinking? Why was he with her when he could have anyone he wanted, not just an exhausted businesswoman on the last leg of a grueling trip?

She didn't see him move and when his fingers curled around her ankle Lana jumped and gasped at the heat flaring from his touch. It singed all the way up her leg and puddled in her belly before reaching down and stirring her deep inside.

He gave her a crooked grin, and her mouth went dry.

He ran his hand up her calf and squeezed. She couldn't tear her gaze from that hand as he moved it along the back of her leg and she shivered when he tickled the sensitive flesh behind her knee. He furthered his trek up to her thigh, sliding his fingers over her skin until all she was aware of was his touch and the throb of need between her thighs. It made her tremble. Lana fell back and closed her eyes.

He took her hand, turning it so the palm faced up, and swirled his thumb lightly over her wrist. She sighed.

"Lana, look at me." She did as he asked.

When their eyes met, her world tipped, and thank God he held her because she needed his touch to ground her. His mouth became her object of obsession. She knew how wonderful those lips were and she was desperate to feel them again. Everywhere.

When his lips moved as he spoke it was as if she were in a dream and his words stilled her heart. "You captivate me."

His low voice was deep, the words so unbelievably sweet. She loved this slow seduction and didn't want him to stop. Liked how cherished it made her feel.

As Grant took her other hand she told herself to reciprocate, but she couldn't. It was as if he'd removed her ability to send messages from brain to muscle.

She gave up trying when his other hand whispered over her bare arm and his fingers curled around the back of her neck. Their gazes locking, he gave a gentle tug, pulling her to him. So close. Oh, so close. The heated tension in air between them seemed to hum with a life of its own, and then it was gone as her breasts pressed against his chest. He cradled the back of her neck while his other hand slipped around her waist and held her captive. Heaven.

"Lana," he murmured, "I haven't been able to get you out of my mind all day."

A contented smile curved her lips. "Me, too. I kept thinking that this isn't the kind of place to be alone in. Its beauty needs to be shared." Was she babbling? Sure felt like it.

"Yes, I agree. However, I want yours all to myself."

"My what?"

"Your beauty. You."

She didn't know what to say, only that those few simple words were music to her ears.

She was in the arms of a stunning man, on a gorgeous island, in a beach house to die for. Probably for this one night only and that was just fine.

3

HE PULLED HER CLOSER. Lana couldn't look away from his
eyes as they caught the torches' flickering light. Mesmerized by their twinkle, she held her breath waiting
for his lips to touch hers. Slowly, he lowered his face
until she felt the warmth of his flesh. It rushed over her
like a firestorm.

"Ohh…my," she murmured, not trusting what might
come out of her mouth. Keeping control of her trembling muscles was becoming increasingly difficult.

He chuckled, the deep resonance of it rumbling from
his chest. The waves crashing on the beach paled in
comparison to the power he exuded.

"Is there anyone waiting for you back home? Because
I think I might just keep you here."

Lana's eyes opened wide with a momentary flash
of unease, until she saw the teasing glint in those
chocolaty-colored depths. He'd been nothing but a
gentleman so far and she did trust her instincts. Yet
the promise of being kept here was alarming, fright-
ening and, she had to admit, oh, so sexy. Her response
to him from the minute they'd crashed into each other

during the flight had been nothing but electric. Lana shivered, imagining all the good bad things they could get up to.

"Not really." It would take a long while for her to get over Grant once their tryst was over, for any other guy to be worth a second look. "But work is expecting me back."

He smiled. "Ah, so if I decide to keep you here forever someone will come hunting for you?"

Lana nodded. "But right now, I don't care." She gripped his shoulders, her fingers tightening on the solidity of them before sliding around to circle his neck. This brought him closer to her, just where she wanted him.

"You're full of surprises, Ms. Canada."

This time Lana laughed, loving the wildness he had no problem pulling out of her. Grant was exactly how she might picture a sexy surfer boy, but with maturity and strength and muscles and distinction. The *ands* could go on and on. The best was how his passion boiled just below the surface. It was a constant presence she felt with her whole being.

She didn't wait for him to kiss her, and tipped her head until their lips brushed. He groaned; his fingers tightened and she didn't care if it left bruises. She would be marked by him. Lana shivered with delight.

Lana wanted him now. Needed to feel him in her. Running on pure desire, she pulled his head down, opening her mouth against his. When their tongues touched and twined Lana was lost. She gave in to him and what may come. What she hoped would come. Knew would come.

He yanked her closer with a rough tug, and she moaned.

Grant slanted his mouth over hers and she pushed her fingers into his hair, pulling it free from its tie. He smelled masculine and divine, like fine wine, sun, sea mist, coconut…it was glorious.

His lips, hands and demeanor grew more insistent and he pressed her back on the lounge, his mouth never moving away from hers. She had no will to argue and let him do as he wanted with…no, to her. The night grew still around them, the crashing of the waves dimmed and the night birds quieted. The only sound was the pounding of their hearts and gasps of breath.

Lana ran her hand down his back and found the edge of his shirt. She pushed her fingers underneath, loving the solid warmth of his back muscles. He had her head gently clasped between his large hands as he rained kisses along her cheek. He turned her head and found her earlobe, teasing it before pressing his lips into the curve of her shoulder, tickling her with a feather-light touch. Lana's head dropped back and a soft sigh escaped her lips.

He moved his knee to rest between her thighs, the lounge groaning under them. The weight of his hips pressing against her wasn't enough. Lana reached down and grabbed his ass, digging her nails into the fabric of his shorts to pull him tighter. He was hard for her and Lana wanted him closer. With no clothing between them.

He slowly pulsed his hips and she felt every ridge of him through the fabric. Lana whimpered with building frustration and she lifted her knees, jamming her heels into the backs of his thighs so she could force him closer. Even through their layers of clothing, the sensations were mind-blowing. She could hardly imagine how fantastic it would feel when they were finally naked.

Grant pulled away from her and sat back on his knees, gazing down at her, his features still shadowed. Lana's chest rose and fell as she tried to get her breathing back to normal. The torchlight reflected passion glittering in his eyes, which only ignited her further. She rested her hands on his hips and slid them down to his thighs. His muscles bulged, and she felt a deep tremor in him, as if he were holding himself back.

"What are you waiting for?" Lana was beyond propriety now. Well, not that she'd ever really had any to begin with when it came to Grant. She was hot for this man in so many ways and being here with him, like this, seemed utterly perfect.

"To make sure this is what you want." Grant's deep voice filled the gazebo. She could tell he was holding himself back, the strain in his voice giving it a gravelly edge.

Everything froze in time as he stared down at her. Lana wasn't able to draw breath. The intensity she saw on his face proved he wanted her far more than he was showing. Couldn't he see how much she wanted him, too?

"If it wasn't what I wanted, I wouldn't be here." Never had she been more honest. It felt right. He felt right. Even though she'd only just met this man, the thought of not being with him filled her with anxiety.

"I'm glad to hear that."

His fingers trailed down her neck to catch the spaghetti straps at her shoulders, pulling them down. She

freed her arms from the straps, her breasts still covered
by the thin fabric. She glanced down, watching breath-
lessly as his large, tanned hands slipped inside the collar
and over her chest to brush across her skin.

Lana's eyelids fluttered but she forced them to stay
open so she could keep watching what he was doing.
Her nipples tightened as he inched the fabric down,
sending shots of desire straight to her clitoris. She cried
out as he thrust his hips again and his rigid cock moved
against her.

"Stop…" She moaned. He was making her crazy
with sensation and she could barely stand it.

"Really? You want me to stop?"

He leaned down, his mouth inches from her breasts.
Would he ever get her top off? Lana fumbled with the
front of his shirt, trying to undo the buttons. But her
fingers wouldn't perform the way she wanted so she let
her hands drop in surrender.

"No." She struggled to speak. "D-don't stop. Ever."

"I was hoping you'd say that."

Lana nodded. "You're killing me."

"Then let's make it the sweetest death possible."

GRANT HELD HIMSELF above her. She was exquisite. It
had been a totally unexpected delight to meet her on
the plane, experience her fiery passion. The feelings
she evoked in him were too complicated to examine
now. All he wanted to do was make love to her. Give
her pleasure. Enjoy her spirit.

Make her want to stay with him as long as she was
in Hawaii.

He gazed at her flushed face, her pale skin pink
from the sun and her arousal. Her dark hair fanned out

over the brightly colored cushions, catching the flickering light. Her eyelids fluttered, her lashes contrasting against her cheeks. He couldn't stop looking at her. The slender column of her neck pulled his eyes down to her chest, which rose and fell with her jagged breathing.

Grant was mesmerized by the tremble of her breasts underneath her top, her nipples visible against the fabric. It was time to get her undressed. He pulled her top down, watching how her nipples hardened from the friction of the material rubbing over them. She moaned, her excitement turning him on so much that he gritted his teeth in order to stay in control.

One last tug and he drew in a sharp breath when her pink nipples came into view. Grant forced himself not to take one between his lips yet.

She quivered below him, squirming on the cushion. Running the backs of his fingers over her taut belly, liking the way her flesh quivered under his touch, he wanted to feel more of her. When he looked at her ivory skin, he thought it more beautiful than any of the tanned flesh paraded about on the Hawaiian beaches.

His hands hovered over the snap on her shorts as he glanced at her face. She was watching him, her eyes half closed and her lips glistening in the torchlight. Lana smiled, and when her tongue reached out to moisten them again he could no longer hold back. He undid her shorts and raised her bottom. Sitting back so he could pull them down, taking her panties with them. She was fully exposed to him; he gazed at her hungrily, unable to get enough of her extraordinary beauty.

Her curls, as dark as the hair on her head, were trimmed into a narrow strip ending just above the cleft where he saw her clitoris peeking out. Grant placed his hands on her hips. He swept his thumbs over her soft skin, and his gaze dipped to her pussy. He'd never seen a prettier one. One that begged to be loved.

Skimming his hands down to her thighs, he gently pushed them wider until she was fully bared to his gaze. Her lean thighs trembled beneath his hands and he skimmed them over her, barely touching her. He held his fingers just above the crease of her thigh, then softly rested them on either side of her mound with the tips of his thumbs ready to dip into her folds.

Lana arched her back and her soft moan spurred him on. She was ready for him. As he gently parted her, the scent of her arousal rose to him, and he lowered his head to taste her. Her soft dark curls brushed his nose as he swept his tongue against her clitoris.

"Oh my God!" Lana cried out when her hands gripped his hair, pulling it painfully, but he welcomed it. The sharp tugs keeping him focused.

Her breathing came faster and her trembling increased. He knew she was about to come. Setting his own needs aside, which only raged stronger as her excitement increased, he gave her all his attention.

He flicked his tongue over her sensitive nub and pressed his fingers into her slick heat, curling against her G-spot. Lana drew in a big breath, held it, and he felt her body tense. She was his in that moment, the moment before her orgasm would crash over her. He held her in the palm of his hand. Completely responsible for her pleasure. Bracing himself, Grant shifted slightly so he could reach into his pocket for the condom he'd hastily shoved into it earlier.

He wanted to bury himself in her as she was climaxing.

She was close and he was ready. He pulled her clit between his lips and pumped his free hand faster. Lana raised her hips and bounced against him crying out as her orgasm neared. Swiftly, Grant sat back, freed himself and slid the condom on. He took hold of her and lifted her ass onto his thighs, positioning his cock against her. He watched as he pressed into her, her pussy greedily accepting him. Lana's pulsations gripped him as her pleasure was unleashed. He kept his thumb on her clit as he thrust in deep, making sure she'd roll right into another orgasm.

She was tight and hot, gripping him with a ferocity that took his breath away. His balls pulled up and Grant let out a roar as he came. Lana's hands grabbed his arms and she let out another scream just as she climaxed again.

Grant yanked on her hips to bring her tight to him before he doubled over and rolled onto his back, taking her with him so she lay draped across him. Her fragrant hair fanned over his face, her heart pounded in time with his. He wrapped his arms around her and held her tight, not wanting to let her go just yet. Liking too much how well they fit together.

4

LANA OPENED HER EYES. The peaked wooden roof with exposed beams above her was unfamiliar. She turned her head, squinting at the blazing sunlight pouring into the room. The ocean sounded as if it came right up to the bed.

Lana sat up and looked around. Her jaw dropped at the opulence of the room. Beautiful wood walls in a deep honey color skirted the bed, with the exception of the nonexistent wall to the outside. Blinking again, she realized an infinity pool was just steps from where she lay.

Glancing down she drew in a quick breath. She was naked. Then a smile slowly curved her lips and a thrill rushed through her. Now she knew where she was. In Grant's house.

His little grass shack. *Yeah, sure.*

She sat in the huge bed, amidst the decadently soft sheets, tumbled and rumpled from their night of loving. She hugged herself and closed her eyes, letting her thoughts drift back over the previous night. They had made love pretty much from the moment she'd set foot in his house until he carried her up the wide coral steps to this magnificent room.

Falling back into the sheets, Lana stretched, enjoying the way her muscles felt. Did she really have to get up? Or could she luxuriate here in bed and wait to see what was going to happen next?

She needed to find a bathroom, at least. Taking a deep breath she gazed around and spied a door. Flinging the covers aside she padded over and gently pushed it open. Lana nearly swallowed her tongue when she saw the fabulous bathroom. It was almost as big as her apartment. She could easily spend a whole day in here lounging in the huge tub full of bubbles—or in the glass-walled shower that, she now saw, overlooked the surf below.

She chose the shower and stepped in, turning on the multitude of taps. An explosion of water hit her from all sides, like a rain forest storm. She stood under the water and closed her eyes, losing herself in the spray. Her long days of travel washed away and she refused to think of the journey ahead, taking her back home in the days to come.

Swiping the stream of water from her eyes, Lana gazed out at the waves as she scrubbed her body and washed her hair. Never in a million years would she have imagined she'd be in such a place as this. And with a man like Grant. She sucked in a breath and let out a contented sigh.

A movement below caught her attention. Wiping the water from her eyes again, Lana focused and realized someone was watching her from the beach. She scooted back to the corner of the shower, shielding herself from view. Curious, she crept forward until she could see the beach again. The person was gone.

Turning off the water she pulled open the door and stepped out.

"I could've watched you wash yourself all day." A deep and very sexy voice surprised her.

Lana let out a squeak and instinctively covered her breasts and mound with her hands. When she realized it was Grant she relaxed and smiled. "You scared the crap out of me."

"Sorry, love. If you hadn't gotten out of the shower when you did I'd be right in there with you." Grant stepped forward, dropped a soft, butter-yellow towel around her shoulders and pulled her into his arms. "You certainly do smell good."

Lana sighed and leaned into him when he pressed his lips to her temple. "I'm soaked and going to get you all wet."

He chuckled. "I'm used to you getting me all wet now."

Lana blushed. "It's not gentlemanly to point certain things out to a lady." She glanced up at him, her lips curving into seductive smile. "But then, who ever said I was a lady?"

He tossed back his head and let out a great laugh. Lord, this man was sexy. Even his laugh warmed her deep in her belly. The muscles in his neck were strong, corded, his jaw wide and square, and she let her gaze roam over him, unable to get enough. But she shook herself out of her lustful haze.

"So," she said quietly, "I guess I should get dressed so you can take me back to my hotel."

"Are you in a hurry, my lovely? Or do you have a

little more time for me? Perhaps we can have breakfast on the lanai."

"That's very tempting." She smiled, trying to keep her excitement under lock and key. "I think I can find some time for you. After all, the real world seems rather dull after what you've shown me over the past twenty-four hours."

Lana quickly got dressed and ran her fingers through her hair. She looked for some toiletries, smiling when she found a neatly organized drawer with a basket of supplies. She used a few items, hair product, facial moisturizer, deodorant and a toothbrush still in its package.

She was surprised by how comfortable she felt in his presence, whether naked or dressed in yesterday's clothes. There definitely was something special about him that allowed her to feel this way. Or maybe it was because he had no expectations of her. After their holiday fling, she would likely never see him again. That gave her a sharp pang of disappointment.

Regardless, Lana was enjoying pushing aside the pressures of the outside world. She didn't want anything to interrupt their day ahead. She was going to roll with it, see what kind of journey Grant would take her on. It wasn't every day a man like him walked into your life. Lana liked this new feeling. And she liked Grant.

Poking his head around the door he called, "Come on then, we're burning light and have lots to do today."

Lana followed him from the bedroom into a wide hall that seemed vaguely familiar to her. "I don't remember this hall."

Grant curled his arm around her shoulders and pulled her tight into his side as he answered. "Well, we did go to the bedroom from the lanai. So you're right, you haven't seen this hallway."

"Ah, I guess I was way too focused on you." She smiled.

Grant chuckled and took her hand, leading her down the hall.

Recalling their antics from last night excited her. The last thing she wanted was not to remember their loving.

"Is there somebody else here today?" she asked him.

"No, there shouldn't be, except for the staff."

"The staff?" He had staff? Good Lord, just how rich was he?

Grant nodded.

"Because I'm not here much, I have staff taking care of the house and grounds. Why do you ask?"

"I saw somebody on the beach earlier when I was in the shower. Sort of alarmed me because he was looking up in my direction, which made me think he could see me."

"Really? That's not like the staff. They're very discreet." Grant was quiet for a moment before continuing, "I'll look into it. But not to worry, the glass is one way, so no one can see in."

Lana nodded, liking that bit of news. They rounded a corner into the great room. Once again she was awestruck.

"I simply cannot get over how wonderful this is. I could never get sick of looking at this view." Lana waved her hand, indicating the lush gardens that skirted the lanai and fell away to the beach and the endless blue ocean. She let out a deep, contented sigh.

"Sit." Grant pulled out a rattan chair at the glass table. Lana did, staring about her. Everything looked so different in the light of day. Just as spectacular, but with a whole new perspective. Would she be here tonight, to enjoy another evening, or would this be her last day with this exciting and wonderfully sexy man?

"You don't ever get tired of this, do you?" she asked, and watched him move around the table to retrieve a tray laden with all sorts of delights from an ornately carved sideboard.

"Never." Grant set the tray down in the center of the glass table, lifted heavy mugs off it and placed one in front of her. "It would be a shame to not be in awe of nature's beauty. Perhaps tomorrow you'll wake early enough to watch the sunrise with me."

Lana's stomach flip-flopped. He was looking ahead, and he wanted her here in the morning, after all. "Well, I suppose that's possible if you don't keep me up all night again." And she winked at him. Winked! That was something she'd never done before. He seemed to bring that out in her.

He laughed and slid his chair around the table so he could sit beside her. The delicious smell of coffee tickled her nostrils, she curled her fingers around the mug, inhaling the aroma as they looked out to the beach.

"Hawaiian coffee?"

"Kona." He took a sip of the black liquid and sat back with a sigh. "There's nothing in the world like it. Black gold."

Lana reached for the cream and poured a generous dollop in. Lifting the mug she took a sip and nearly died with delight.

"Oh my God, this is the best coffee I've ever had." She took a sip again and glanced at him over the rim of her mug. Now why on earth would he have such a secretive smile? "What? Why are you looking at me like that? It's not like I haven't had coffee before, or Hawaiian coffee. Kona. But I've never had anything taste so good."

"Maybe it has something to do with freshness." He smiled and took a sip of his own.

Lana nodded. "Perhaps there's a better way to ship Hawaiian coffee, keep it fresher for the export market."

"Oh, are you an expert on shipping and product freshness? Is that what you were away on business for?" Grant inquired.

"It's part of what I do. If you want a good product, you need to take care of it while getting it from A to B."

"You're absolutely right, Lana." Grant lifted a plate of what smelled like freshly made biscuits, jam and fresh island fruit off the tray and placed it before them. "It's one of my directives."

"Mm-hm. Wow, this fruit looks wonderful." Lana leaned forward and picked a piece of pineapple out of the bowl. Its juice dripped over her fingers. She put the piece back on the plate and sucked the sweetness off. She realized Grant was watching her lick the sticky syrup off and she blushed. Lana speared the pineapple with her fork and took a bite. She thought she'd died and gone to heaven. It was the best pineapple she'd ever tasted. "What with coffee, the pineapple, the view, what more could a girl ask for?"

"Anything your heart desires." Grant took a biscuit and Lana watched as he chewed and took another bite. The muscles in his jaw were just as powerful as the rest of him.

"Anything, huh?"

"That's what I said." Grant gave her a slow wink, and her belly did a little tumble.

"Well, if you want me to hang around, I'm game. I've never been to Hawaii before and I would be ready to see anything—" she paused and gave him a steady look "—or do anything. I'd also be very content to stay here and enjoy the view. I'm easy."

His eyes met hers over the rim of his coffee cup, blond brows arching. He put the cup down, pushed his chair back and stood up. "It seems rather silly to me to stay here all day when there's a big, beautiful island to explore."

Lana took another sip of the wonderful coffee and set her mug down. "Okay, then. Shall we?"

She stood and held out her hand to Grant. He took it, and the next thing she knew they were roaring down his driveway in a Jeep with the top down. Lana hung on to the dashboard and laughed out loud when her hair whipped around her face from the wind as they took off down the road.

5

Banzai Pipeline was usually a hit for most visitors. Grant made it a stop whenever he was on island. The waves were smaller now than during the winter, but still very impressive. If they were lucky there might be a few surfers out there to watch.

"How about we stop here and grab a few things for our trip around the island?"

He pulled into the lot of an old local bakery.

"Wow, how long has this place been here?"

"Long time. It's a great spot with good food. Since it's early in the morning, and you didn't have a whole lot for breakfast I thought we'd pick up some pastries to tide us over until we eat later." Grant held the door for Lana and followed her inside. It was a great place to meet locals, surfers and, of course, tourists. They'd been carrying his coffee for a while and Grant liked to give back business to his customers.

He watched Lana beeline to the display of baked goods.

"Wow, these look amazing. I could easily gain a hundred pounds coming in here. I'll have one of everything, please." She laughed and took a step closer to Grant as he came beside her. He dropped his arm around her shoulders and gave her a hug.

"Is something calling your name?"

"I wouldn't know where to begin. It all looks so yummy. Since you're familiar with the place, what do you recommend?" Lana smiled at him and it was as if the sun had just filled the room with golden light. Grant felt like sweeping her into his arms right there and kissing her until she was breathless. There was something about her easy nature that made him feel comfortable. Like he didn't always have to be on guard. Plus, he was sure she had no idea the sexuality she radiated. Being near her kept him in a simmering state of arousal.

"All right, then." He turned to the girl behind the counter. "We'll have a piece of the pineapple macadamia nut cheesecake, lilikoi cheese pie, one each cornbread and brownie with two large Americano coffees."

"Holy, Grant, that's a lot of goodies. I won't be able to eat all that."

"Trust me, you won't let any of this go to waste. It's the best you'll ever taste. And if we don't eat it, we take it home and throw it in the fridge." They could enjoy something more savory later. For sunset. He had a plan for this evening and needed to make a phone call to set it up.

He followed Lana out the door, watching the sexy sway of her ass in her white shorts. He couldn't wait to get her back into bed. Grant usually moved on after a night with a woman, not wanting any complications. He never had breakfast with them. Ever. His divorce had burned too badly. That Lana didn't seem to know who he was eased his mind. Being the owner of King'ha Coffee made him cautious. Especially with his expansion plans. So far, he wasn't getting any indication Lana was a gold digger. She appeared in control of her own destiny and content to spend time together, but that didn't mean he'd let his guard down.

A mile or so down the road they stopped at the pipeline and stayed in the Jeep under the overhang of palm trees and hibiscus.

"This is impressive," Lana commented. "I've heard of the Banzai Pipeline before but never realized just how…gosh, I don't even know how to describe it. Dramatic! Those waves are huge."

Grant took the pies out of the bag. "The waves are bigger in the winter and are starting to ease up now. If you think these are huge, wait until you see them in January."

Did I just make a plan for nine months from now? He took a quick look at Lana to see if she'd picked up on that, but she was still staring out over the water. Had she heard him? If she did, she wasn't letting on. What had happened to the caution he was adamant about?

"Okay, so we have two completely different pies here. Take a bite from each one and tell me which one you'd rather eat."

She swung her gaze to the treats he held out. She touched her tongue to her top lip as she tried to decide. Grant's groin tightened thinking of her pink, wet tongue licking his cock.

"I can never make a decision when it comes to stuff like this." She sighed, then bit her lower lip. Her concentration on which piece of decadence to eat charmed him. She glanced up at him, her eyes dark and mysterious. "How about we each eat half and then trade? That way we don't have to choose."

Grant smiled and cut the pieces in half. "I guess it can be hard to choose sometimes. Depending what those choices are."

Keeping his gaze on hers, Grant leaned over, unable to deny himself a quick kiss. Her eyes widened as he covered her mouth with his. Her lips opened, and that was all he needed as an invitation. He found her tongue with his, tasting and pulling it into his mouth. Liking the soft moan that came from deep in her throat.

His thigh muscle clenched when her hand rested on him. Her palm was warm, electrifying against his flesh, and when she slipped her fingertips underneath the edge of his shorts, he was all but ready to forget about the bakery treats.

A siren screamed behind them as an ambulance raced past, shattering their intimate moment. Breathless, Lana sat back and blinked, her eyes glazed with desire. Grant knew it would be way too easy for them to get carried away out here under the tropical trees.

"That was an ambulance." Lana craned her neck to see where it had gone, her breathing still ragged.

"Yeah, not a good sign when you're up by the pipeline."

"I imagine people could get hurt a lot here."

He nodded. "It's not a place for those who don't have experience."

Grant shifted in his seat and handed her the box of goodies.

Lana speared the point of a slice of pie and popped it into her mouth. Her eyes closed and she let out a very sultry groan, an echo of the noises she made last night. "This is amazing. What a good call to make a stop here."

Grant savored a bite of his own. "Yes, this place has been a landmark for many years."

"Normally I'm not a dessert person, but this could definitely change my way of thinking." She tasted the other piece of pie and gasped. "Wow. And I have a party in my mouth! What an explosion of flavor, love it."

He laughed and dug in to his piece. It wasn't hard to pass the next few minutes in silence as they ate and drank the coffee. The brownie and cornbread could easily wait until they needed a snack later on. The sun was higher in the sky and it was time to get going.

She took a sip of her coffee and then turned to him. "What are the chances of two good cups of coffee in such a short period of time?"

"The bakery has the same kind of coffee I had this morning."

"Is that so? What, are you a coffee tycoon or something?"

There. The perfect opportunity. Yet he hesitated, still unable to let his guard down. It would be easy to tell her he'd made his fortune in Hawaiian coffee and in the thousands of coffee shops scattered across New Zealand, Australia and South Africa. About his expansion plans into the US and Canada. But if he told her, then she'd know who he was, and that could change everything. He wasn't sure if he was ready for that level of openness. Yet. He wanted, needed, to get to know her a little better. He wanted her to know the real him. Money had a strange way of clouding the issue.

Instead of answering her, he laughed and put the Jeep in gear. He didn't like not being honest with her but he'd been burned once by a woman he had trusted. Plus, it was rather nice to live in anonymity for a change. With no worries.

"So, what do you have up your sleeve for the day?"

Grant rested his wrist on top of the steering wheel and reached across to take her hand with his free one.

"We'll just tour the island and stop anywhere you feel like stopping. Maybe end up taking in a sunset."

Which reminded him he had to make that phone call.

LANA WATCHED LUSH foliage rush past them as they drove down the road. He'd made a few references to the future, the sunset tonight, even the waves next January. It would be easy to fall into the trap of thinking about tomorrow with him. Her scheduled time here was only brief. Was it fair to spend the whole time with him? She had work to do, which she should be doing now! And what about him? He had a business to run, too.

Lana didn't want to be a leech, but he sure made her want to spend time with him, enjoy another morning waking up in his bed. She turned to Grant and watched him drive for a few minutes before asking, "Who do you think that guy I saw on the beach was?"

He shrugged. "Hard to say. All our beaches are public. We don't get too many people out front of my place, but it does happen. Are you a sun worshipper?"

"Not really. I like to be outside, and I wear lots of sunscreen, but it's hard for me to just lie in the sun and do nothing. If I get a tan it's usually from hiking, swimming or just being outside. Do you spend time outside? Surfing?"

He was tanned, but not super dark, and she could tell he was outdoorsy. Not just from his muscular physique—he had fine lines around his eyes that crinkled up when he laughed. Totally charming. All perfect to go with his blond hair. He could totally pull off surfer boy.

He laughed out loud and she wondered what was so funny.

"No, I don't have a death wish anymore. I surfed when I was younger, but wasn't that great at it. You may have noticed this." He pulled up the leg of his shorts and pointed to the scar she'd seen last night. "Reef damage."

"That's quite a battle scar." She placed her palm over the jagged, healed-up flesh. A tremor ran through him when their skin touched and she glanced at him.

"My days of being an adrenaline junkie and doing pretty much anything to get a high are long gone. My brother carries that torch."

Adrenaline junkie and crazy brother. How interesting. She pondered those tidbits, which made him even more intriguing. She'd wondered about his career. What he did that allowed him to have a beach house, fly first class and seem to live a carefree lifestyle.

She reminded herself that she'd just met Grant yesterday. Or was it two days ago? She never could keep the days and hours straight after crossing the international dateline. Either way, Grant was a mystery. One she had a notion to solve.

6

"THIS IS INSANE!" Lana cried, and stared out the window as the Bell 407 tour helicopter took a sharp bank over the shoreline below. Spectacular beaches were tucked in between the lava flows spread underneath them, and she placed her palms on the window, bracing herself even though she was wearing a four-point harness. The sensation of flying overcame her and she let out a whoop, nothing but the glass between her and the vista below. She turned to Grant. "I wish I had my camera," Lana shouted into the microphone of the headset she wore.

"Nothing better than memories to take with you." His voice, coming through her earpiece, was comforting and deep.

The *whomp whomp* of the helicopter blades thudded up through the seats, creating a bass backdrop for the majestic view.

Lana turned back to the window, in awe of the vista below. They'd leveled out and finished the turn. The last thing she ever expected was this little jaunt over to the Big Island of Hawaii. Grant had been mysterious about making a phone call earlier today; clearly he'd been planning this surprise. He'd told Lana a good friend owned a helicopter tour company, so he'd made arrangements for them to be picked up in Honolulu and flown to Kona for this sunset tour.

When they'd zipped low over the water in the open-door helicopter on the flight between the islands, it had been exhilarating. The helicopter they were in now was far more luxurious than that one, almost like a limo.

Lana had no clue what the rest of the night would entail, but being with Grant was all that mattered. She reached over and took his hand, never looking away from the window, and he tightened his fingers around hers. A sense of contentment swelled inside her. Grant filled every minute of her thoughts. Had it really only been a couple of days since they met?

"I've never seen anything so spectacular in all my life." She craned her neck so as not to miss a thing as they flew toward the volcano.

The pilot's voice came through the earpieces. "Take a look below. With the sun behind the mountain you can get a good look at the lava and magma lake in Halema'uma'u Crater. Beyond that we'll fly over the Punalu'u black sand beach and Punalu'u green sand beach."

"Green sand? I've never heard of such a thing," Lana exclaimed.

"It gets its color from the olivine crystals created from eruptions of a dormant volcano a whole lot of years ago."

Lana fell quiet, completely in awe. She took a quick glance at Grant, who was watching her rather than looking outside. Impulsively she leaned over and gave him a quick kiss before focusing on the view again, drawing in a breath when she saw the orange glow from the lava.

"This is magnificent."

"The sun will be setting soon, and you don't want to miss that," the pilot advised.

The pilot provided a narrative for the tour. "New land is made when the lava hits the ocean. You may have noticed the coffee farms at the beginning of our flight. There are a few, and I'm sure you'll see the oldest one later. Grant should—"

The deep timbre of Grant's voice interrupted the pilot. "The sun is setting, Lana. You don't want to miss it. I doubt we'll see a green flash today with the clouds on the horizon."

They flew just above the puffy softness of the clouds. She forgot about the island and the volcano behind her as the magic of the sunset ahead of them filled her with wonder. She had no words for the vision of the sky streaked with pinks and oranges. All she could do was gasp and watch as the colors shifted to deep tones of blazing red and purple.

"Look behind us, Lana."

She turned her head, sucked in a breath and whispered, "Oh my God."

The view behind them was just as spectacular, the clouds stained from the reflection of the sunset. She couldn't have been more surprised when her eyes filled with tears. Grant squeezed her hand and she turned to look at him, a huge lump in her throat.

"Thank you. I've never been more moved by nature."

Grant smiled and leaned forward, catching the tear on her cheek with his thumb. "It was my pleasure to see you enjoy yourself. I'm glad you're happy."

She nodded. Strangely, she didn't feel at all ashamed or self-conscious that it had made her cry. When she could speak without a catch in her voice, Lana told him, "These past two days with you have been totally unexpected, and I've loved every minute. I don't know how to thank you."

His smile widened and her heart lurched a little.

"I'm sure I could think of something." Grant winked and Lana burst out laughing.

As IF THE day could get any better, a car was waiting for them when the helicopter landed to whisk them away to a very exclusive luau. When they arrived Grant handed her off to a group of ladies who carefully outfitted her in the most gorgeous native Hawaiian outfit. She couldn't believe the vision that stared back at her when she looked in the mirror.

Lana turned her head to see the lei po'o of exquisite pink and yellow frangipani they'd placed on her head and how it contrasted with her dark hair. Not to mention the to-die-for scent that she would never get enough of. Matching flower Kupe'e encircled her wrists and ankles, and a necklace of polished nuts hung about her shoulders. The ti leaf skirt hung low on her hips and ended at her knees. A flesh-toned bikini-style top made it look as if her breasts were naked.

The ladies then shooed her down an outdoor pathway through an arched ceiling of palm fronds. Grant waited for her at the end. He had changed his clothes as well, and now stood shirtless, barefoot and wearing a decorated loincloth. Lana's mouth dried up when she saw him. It made her realize that she hadn't really seen him without his clothes on. Last night the lights had been low, and then they'd been under the covers.

His hair was loose and he also wore a lei po'o, but

his seemed more masculine, made of forest greens. His shoulders were broad and strong. Her gaze hungrily traveled over his muscled chest, dusted with just enough hair, down to his hips. Her belly fluttered when she saw the ridges on either side of his hips disappear beneath his loincloth. Good Lord, his legs were fantastic, his thighs muscled and bulging as he shifted feet, his rough thigh scar didn't detract from his deliciousness. Even his calves were beautiful. He was heart stopping, and right about now, if they'd been anywhere but here, she'd have crawled all over him.

Instead, Lana swallowed and put on her best sexy saunter, swayed her hips and let the spirit take her. Perhaps she could get him as turned on for her as she was for him, building the sexual tension until...well, just until. Later.

"C'mere, gorgeous." Grant wrapped her in a big hug, his hands sliding over her bare back and pulling her flush so they were skin to skin.

There was no mistaking the bulge that pushed against her, which only skyrocketed her arousal. Tipping her head back she gazed up into his eyes and placed a hand on his cheek. She tugged him down so that their lips met in a gentle kiss, which, she knew, could erupt at any moment into volcanic explosion.

Sliding her arms around his neck she lifted her head enough so that she was able to murmur against him. "This has been the best day of my life. I hope it has for you, too."

Grant led her along a path resplendent with tropical foliage, towering palm trees and the sweet scent of flowers. It was pure heaven.

"It's almost time for the call-to-feast celebration."

"What's that?" Lana asked, snuggling in tighter to him.

"It's the nightly ceremonial torch lighting. Have you ever seen the movie *Blue Hawaii* with Elvis Presley? They show it in that movie."

"No, I haven't. But I guess I'll be looking for it when I get home."

"An old resort on Kauai did it nightly until a hurricane devastated the place back in the 1990s. They replicate the event here. First we'll be called to gather by the blowing of a conch shell. And then a runner goes through the grounds, swinging a flame at the end of a rope so that it hits each torch on the ground, lighting it. It's quite spectacular."

"It sounds—oh! Is that what you mean?"

A low-pitched, haunting keen filled the air, sending shivers down Lana's spine.

"Yes. Quite lovely, isn't it."

"It gives me goose bumps. Are we close? I don't want to miss the torch lighting."

Grant chuckled and squeezed her shoulders. "Just up ahead now."

They emerged from the tropical tunnel of flowers to stand in front of a low wall made of stone or coral. A few people dressed similarly to them had gathered there, some holding wineglasses and others coconuts with straws. Lana was enraptured by the view of the darkened palm grove beyond the wall and the lagoon in front of them. Everything was hushed, making Lana hold her breath. Even the night birds were still.

"Stand in front of me," Grant instructed, his voice a whisper. She stood with her knees pressed against the wall and Grant sandwiching her from behind. He slipped his arms around her waist, his fingers softly brushing the skin on her stomach. Lana curled her fingers around his forearm and hugged him tighter, anxiously waiting for the show to begin.

The conch shell blew again and then a male voice shouted out a chant. Moments later the night air was filled with the throbbing beat of Hawaiian drums. Lana's heart nearly burst with emotion at the sight before her. A Hawaiian man dressed in traditional clothes emerged, swinging a ball of fire on the end of a rope. Then he started to run in time with the beat of the drums. On every second swing he somehow managed to hit one of the torches on the ground. Each burst into flame as he continued to the next one and the next, sprinting through the breathtaking palm grove until all the torches were lit, creating an ethereal sight.

"Oh, Grant. First a night at your beautiful house, then a day exploring the island, a helicopter ride, then the sunset and now this." Lana turned in his arms. "I've never been shown a better time. I swear, I'll never forget this as long as I live."

He smiled, showing a dimple on his left cheek she hadn't noticed before, and her heart melted. Lana reached up and pushed her fingers through his hair, guiding his head down to her, desperate to feel his lips on hers, but he pulled back.

"Easy now, there'll be time for that later, trust me. Now we must find our seats. Whilst you were being readied, I made sure we had a prime table."

Lana blinked and shook her head, bringing herself back to the present. Yes, they had all night. But the night started now.

They followed the other guests down a sandy path and emerged onto a wide beach. The sun had long since set, and the shoreline was scattered with torches flickering in the evening breeze off the sea. Delicious aromas wafted around them, making Lana's mouth water. The bakery treats were a distant memory, and she was famished.

They followed a gorgeous young woman with a body to die for to their knee-high table set before the stage. Covered in kappa cloth, its surface was decorated by tropical flowers and leaves, with candles tucked among them. Colorful cushions were arranged on a blanket over the sand for them to sit on. Lana curled her legs under her and leaned against the handy backrest. Grant settled beside her and pulled her close. It was quite cozy.

"I'm guessing you've never been to a luau before, ya?"

Lana smiled, still unaccustomed to his South African accent, and shook her head. "No, I haven't. This is my first trip to Hawaii."

"Then you are in for a treat." He reached for the pitcher on the table in front of them and filled her glass. "This is one of the better luaus in the Hawaiian Islands—exclusive, private, discreet. And the food is top-notch."

"What do you mean 'discreet'?" Lana inquired, but somehow she knew.

His lips beside her ear and his breath fluttering her hair, he said, "Pretty much anything your heart desires can be attained here."

Lana sat up and looked around, taking in the groups of people scattered in front of the stage. She hadn't really noticed how seductively everyone was dressed. Looking at the couples and groups, she could see the sexuality and romance oozing from them. The air was thick with anticipation. Surprisingly, it didn't make her feel self-conscious in the least, only more aroused.

The first course arrived and Grant explained the dishes laid out before them. She gave up trying to remember all the different foods but made sure to taste everything. There was nothing, except perhaps the poi, that she wasn't fussy on.

The entertainment on stage was traditional and quite beautiful. Lana loved the drums and the voices and the dancers. The fire dance was stunning, and by the time it was over she was sated, had a nice buzz from the mai tais and was very content curled up next to Grant.

"Don't get too comfortable yet, my lovely. The best part is yet to come."

Before Lana could ask what he meant, a handsome Polynesian man came and took her hand. Grant helped push her to her feet and when she turned to him he nodded his head to the stage.

"Go on then. Show me what you've got." His smile was contagious and she returned it having no idea what lay in store for her.

She let herself be led to the stage, along with a few other women dressed like she was. A lovely woman, tanned and lean, stood before them in an elaborate Hawaiian dress. Her skirt was made from strands of shells that hung to her knees, and two highly polished coconut shells, held together with the thinnest of strings, covered her breasts. She wore an elaborate spray of feathers on her head. When she did a graceful turn before them, Lana saw a matching spray of feathers in the center of the waistband right over her bottom. Her black hair hung to her hips and when she was facing the women once again, her beautiful smile was infectious.

"Now, ladies, please watch me and I will teach you a few simple moves so you can dance for your man."

Lana's heart leaped to her throat. She was never a great dancer, but damn if she wasn't going to give this a good old college try. The drums started, and the thumping, rhythmic beat got into her blood. She was dumbstruck watching the seductive, hypnotic moves of their instructor. The hula dance was beautiful, sensual and fluid. Lana found herself completely enjoying this experience, trying her best to be as graceful as their teacher.

Then it was their turn to show their stuff.

GRANT WAS VERY pleased with the day. Lana appeared to love everything they'd done and now, with her up on stage, he couldn't wait to see how she moved. He was lucky that Dan, his friend and owner of Sunset Tours, had had a helicopter available to whisk them to the Big Island. And then having space at Paradise Luau was even better.

He kept his eyes on the stage, watching all the ladies practice, smiling to see how happy Lana was. He took a deep breath. Tonight they'd go to his house on this island. She would be the first woman, other than his ex-wife, to see it. Amanda had tried to get his island homes in the divorce settlement, but no way was he going to allow that. She'd hated Hawaii, complained every time they went that she'd rather be anywhere else. But she'd tried to get the houses in the settlement because she knew how much he loved them. He'd never imagined when they first married that she could be so spiteful, but he'd learned quickly. The only thing he could thank her for was his wariness around other women.

But seeing Lana laughing and swinging her hips on

the stage…well, maybe not all women had an agenda. He picked up his glass and tossed back the mai tai in one big gulp. Then reached for the pitcher to fill up both their glasses. Lana seemed genuine, down-to-earth, and her reaction to the sunset helicopter ride had surprised him. She seemed able to live in the moment.

The drums' rising beat echoed under the banyan leaves. The ladies lined up across the stage, and his gaze met Lana's. Her face was flushed and her violet eyes sparkled in the flickering light. Her hands hung by her sides as she slowly swayed her hips. Grant wondered if she realized she was doing it or was just feeling the music, allowing it to get inside her as much as it did him. She blew him a kiss and winked. That spunky little gesture made his heart jump, which surprised the hell out of him.

This woman was electric and he couldn't wait to see her move in time with the drums.

She didn't break eye contact with him as she raised her arms in perfect time with the other women. She lifted her heels, bent her knees, made her hips swing while she moved her arms and fingertips in a gentle wave. Turning and really shaking her hips, she glanced over her shoulder before facing him again. Her breasts jiggled in the skimpy top and her belly was perfection.

Grant touched his lips with his tongue, remembering how good she'd tasted last night. Her sensual dance turned him on in no time, his cock hardening with the promise of what was to come. He dropped a hand into his lap to keep himself from potential exposure, the whole time not looking away from Lana.

She reached her arms in front of her and turned her

hands palms up, using her fingers to beckon him before turning, working her hips so her ass shook deliciously under the skirt, and then faced him again. The crescendo of drums ended abruptly and silence filled the grounds before applause erupted around him.

When she finally descended the steps he stood to greet her. Her eyes dropped to his groin and she smiled. He no longer cared—all he could think about was getting her back to his house so they could make love.

"What did you think?" Her excitement was contagious.

"You were fantastic. I couldn't look away." Pulling her down, they tumbled onto the pillows. He pressed his hips against her so she could tell how turned on he was before sealing his lips over hers.

She kissed him back, her arms around his neck holding him tight. Grant raised his head and looked at her. "Let's get out of here."

She nodded, her eyelids heavy with passion. "But where can we go?"

"I have a surprise for you."

"Oh, Grant. Haven't you given me enough surprises today? This is getting too much, it's overwhelming."

"Are you complaining?" He smirked, stood and reached for her hand to help her up.

She shook her head, catching the exotic scent of the flowers in her hair. "Not at all, it's just you're giving me so much. How can I thank you?"

"Didn't you ask me that earlier?" He led her back to their car. "But you're not getting out of that outfit, until later of course. I want you to dance for me again."

7

"My, my, my. Whose house is this?" Lana was dumb-struck. It seemed she was traveling in the rich-folk stratosphere. "This is absolutely stunning."

Grant walked across the highly polished wood floor to drop the bag with their clothing on a sand-colored chair. Clearly this home had been professionally decorated. Either that or the owner had impeccable taste.

"Do you like it?" Grant asked as he approached her.

"Yes! It's gorgeous." She turned to look out the tall, vast windows that ran the length of the room. "This isn't on the beach though, is it?"

"No, we're up the mountain a bit. On one of the coffee plantations. In fact, the oldest one."

She turned to face Grant. He'd come up behind her and slipped his arms around her waist. "So we get to spend the night here and have great coffee in the morning again, eh?"

He laughed.

"That's the first Canadian-ism I've heard you say. 'Eh.'"

"Well no different than your South African twang, 'whilst' this and 'ya' that." She giggled, liking how they seemed to be able to tease each other. "But I like it. It's sexy."

"Ah, I see. So whilst I'm making love to you, I should speak so you can hear my South African accent, ya?"

"Most definitely!" Lana slipped out of his arms and walked to the windows, purposefully swaying her hips as she searched for a sliding door. "Here we go...oh my God, even in the dark the view is something else."

"You can't see anything, just the lights of the houses in town below."

"I know, but the way they twinkle, and the moon over the water, and look—" she gasped and pointed "—there's a ship out there, too."

"We get lots of cruise ships through here."

Lana shivered when Grant's warm hands gently grasped her shoulders. He massaged her softly and ran his fingers along the tops of her shoulders up her neck, then back down to grasp her upper arms. He turned her until they stood face-to-face.

"Haven't we done enough sightseeing for one day?" Grant inquired, and she was caught in the chocolaty softness of his gaze.

Lana nodded and swallowed. Her stomach tumbled over itself, and even though they'd spent the day together grabbing kisses and touches whenever they could, things were about to get much more serious.

"Do you know your way around this house? Maybe you can find a bedroom."

"Ya, I do." Grant lifted her into his arms. "But I have a much better place in mind."

Lana wound her arm around his shoulder and snuggled into his chest. Still in their little costumes, their bare flesh touched and she sighed as his dusting of hair tickled her. In his arms she felt safer than she ever had in all her life.

She didn't care where he was taking her, as long as they were together. She closed her eyes and rested her head on his shoulder, enjoying being wrapped up in his arms. She heard the whisper of a sliding door but she kept her eyes closed until he instructed her to open them. She did and gasped.

"Oh, it's an infinity pool!"

Grant let her legs go, holding her tight to his chest, her toes dangling next to him. She kept her arms wrapped around his neck, looking up into his eyes. "Another beautiful house. You must know so many people to have pulled off a day like today."

He smiled and the dimple deepened in his cheek. "I have my connections." He lowered his head to her and she watched him descend. When their lips touched, her eyelids fluttered closed and she lost herself in the sensation of their kiss. She opened her mouth to him, her tongue touching his. Unable to deny the arousal roaring through her she pulled his head roughly down to her, tighter, not wanting him stop.

Grant let her slide down his body slowly, her breasts against his chest, her hips against his, his cock pressing her belly until her toes touched the floor. His large hand slid down her back and grasped her ass, pulling her snug to him. She moaned into his mouth and they stood as if fused.

His hands seemed to be everywhere on her at once. The bikini top fell away and excitement trilled through her when her breasts finally came in full contact to his chest. He pushed down the skirt, which dropped with a rustle of leaves around her ankles. His mouth never left hers. She hooked her thumbs through the waist of his loincloth, then slid her hands around to the front and dipped them beneath the fabric.

She needed to feel him, his hardness, the length of him. Closing her fingers around his cock, she tightened, liking how it throbbed in her hand as she stroked him, up and down, and then up along the ridge of him to rub her palm over his cock head. She cradled his balls with her other hand, gently kneading them, and gave a throaty laugh when he dropped his hands from her body as if in supplication, giving her power over him.

With a quick push, she had his loincloth to his feet, and for the first time he stood completely naked before her. No undone shirt, or bedcovers or darkness hid his body this time. Lana stepped back and let her gaze wander over him. The passion in his eyes was for her, and her heart raced, almost making it hard to breathe. But she didn't want to look away from him, loving the wide muscular shoulders that gave way to the firm planes of his chest. His tan contrasted with his blond hair. She'd never before been with a man who had such a perfect body and she was awed. Her fingers itched to brush over the hardness of his stomach and follow that delightful ridge on either side of his hips lower to her prize. His cock jutted proudly from his body.

Lana dropped to her knees, and placed her hands on the knot of scar tissue on his thigh, her lips following with the desire to kiss away any pain he may still have. Inching forward on her knees, she slid her hands higher and slipped her fingers into the soft curls at the base of his cock. Encircling the root she ran her hands along the length of him, squeezing gently at the end. Licking her lips, she pressed the tip of his cock to her mouth. It flexed in her hands as she pushed her lips past the head, flattening her tongue along the underside and flicking it across the thick vein. Grant's fingers curled around the back of her neck, tightening and releasing as she sucked and drew him more into her mouth.

His thighs trembled and Lana wrapped her arms around his hips, gripping his firm butt. Grant started a slow and gentle thrust, meeting her when she slipped down farther on his cock. He was large, and she relaxed, wanting to take him as deeply as she could, desperate to give him back the pleasure he'd made sure she'd experienced every other time. This time was for him.

"Lana, keep that up and…ahh."

She swirled her tongue around the tip and rapidly flicked it on his sensitive glans. She felt his ass muscles contract and the quivering in his legs increased. She wanted him to come. His cock thickened in her mouth and she knew it would be soon. Sliding her hand forward, she cradled his balls, liking how they pulled up tight. She let his cock pop out of her mouth and swirled her tongue around, dipping it into the tiny hole at the tip before gobbling him again. She used her other hand to slide up and down the length, alternating with tight squeezes and fast pumps.

Grant's breathing became rougher, as did the thrust of his hips. He was all male, animalistic in his response to her, and Lana loved it. Loved that she could have such profound power over a strong and commanding man. He was all hers, in the palm of her hand from the magic of her lips on him. He sucked in a breath and groaned, deep and long. He grasped her hair and it pulled between his fingers, the sharp tug almost pleasurable as her own arousal ramped up in time with his.

Petals fell from the lei po'o as he got rougher, their sweet scent surrounding them in a sultry tropical world. Lana moaned, working her lips, her tongue, her hands, until he tensed and let out a roar as he came. She held him tight, drawing out his pleasure until he staggered on his feet, his breath coming in great gulps.

He gently pulled her off him and lifted her up until he had her wrapped in his arms again.

"You'll kill me, woman." Grant pressed a tender kiss to her forehead and Lana sighed.

"Just giving you sweet payback. Now, how about we take a dip?" she whispered against his neck, warmth and his male scent enveloping her.

"Your wish is my command."

Grant carried her into the pool. Arching ripples ringed out across the pristine surface to roll over the edge into infinity. He let her go and she sank into the water.

"Oh, this is lovely and cool." Turning onto her back she floated toward the edge.

Grant dove under, creating a splash, and a spray of water cascaded over her. He popped up beside her, his hair slicked back, showing his high forehead and strong brow.

"You're a mermaid. Look how the moon glistens off your wet skin." He ran a finger up her belly, between her breasts before touching an engorged nipple where it peeped above the surface.

A shiver ran through her when he tweaked her nipple, shots of electric fire raced through her blood, zeroing in on her clit. She rolled over and paddled to the edge, hoping, wanting—knowing—he'd follow her.

She placed her elbows on the edge, marveling how

the pool's boundary hardly seemed as though it was there. The water flowed over the rounded glass side into a trough about three feet down that ran the length of the pool. Looking over, she saw a garden of sorts clinging to the wall, also spanning the length of the trough. Beautiful flowers spilled over as a canopy to a lanai below.

She smiled, warmth rushing through her body when Grant snuggled up behind her, pinning her to the side of the pool.

"This is nice." Lana leaned her head back on Grant's shoulder.

"Yes it is. One of my favorite places."

She nodded, and then it dawned on her. "One of your favorite places? Do you come here often?"

"Whenever I get the chance. Sadly, not often enough." He pressed his lips to the curve of her neck, invoking delightful tremors.

Lana tipped her head sideways, giving him more access. He ran his tongue up to her ear.

"W-what do you mean…ahh, Grant." She blinked, trying to focus, and her fingers grasped his forearms, which had tightened like a band just under her bare breasts.

He kissed her just behind the ear and murmured. His hands rose and cupped her breasts beneath the water. She moaned as his thumbs swept over her hardened nipples, encouraging them to rise up. Desire filled her at a luxuriously maddening speed. Lana gave up on rational thought. Her body wanted to feel, not think. So she abandoned trying to think and gave in to the feelings racing through her.

His cock, hard and insistent, bumped against her ass cheeks. She reached behind her, taking him in her hand

and sliding up and down his length, slick with the water around them. Grant lowered a hand to inch down her belly, stopping for a moment to play with her belly button before moving lower until his finger pushed on her clitoris for the briefest of seconds. Then his fingers traveled lower, sliding through her folds to find her core. He crooked his fingers and found his way into her, the heel of his hand working in time with his thrusts on her clit.

She didn't want to come without his cock in her and held back, even though she was rocketing toward an orgasm.

"Grant." She panted and twisted in his arms to face him. She pressed her lips to his cheek. "How can we? Without protection."

He cupped her face in his hands and Lana's heart swelled at the look in his eyes. "I trust you. Trust me. I've been tested and alone for a long time."

Lana sighed and tightened her arms around him. "Oh, me, too. I've stayed on birth control, waiting, hoping to find someone…"

Grant groaned and claimed her lips in a fierce, demanding kiss. Moments later Lana lifted her head, breathless.

"I want you in me. I've been waiting all day and night to feel your cock stretch me." Lifting her legs, Lana wrapped around his hips, not at all shy. Reaching between them she guided him until the tip of his cock reached her opening. Their gazes locked, Lana tangled her fists in his hair and pulled his head down to her. The dark passion in his eyes surely matched her own.

Grant reached for her, his thumbs resting along her chin, his fingers in her hair. His body quaked and it was as if he was coming unleashed. How could he be hard again so quickly? The thought fled as she was overcome with pleasure. He was all that mattered. Grant's teeth gritted and his brows furrowed, all the while he never looked away from her.

"Now, Grant. Don't make me wait—"

She let out a surprised scream when at last he thrust deep into her, slamming her back against the glass side of the pool. He still held her between his hands so she couldn't turn away or bury her face in his neck, only watch him. And they made love with a fury that turned the water around them from an infinity of calmness into a boiling cauldron.

She barely heard the water slosh over the side into the trough below, she was so fixated on Grant and the excruciating heaven he created as her orgasm built. She closed her eyes, and visions of them together last night, today, her dancing for him and the passion etched on his face as he watched her filled her mind, carrying her faster and faster to her place of approaching bliss.

She matched him thrust for thrust, locking her heels behind his back. Grant reached between them, finding her clit until she was quivering in his arms.

"You're shaking."

His voice filled her ear and she licked her lips, nodding quickly. "I—I know…can't help it."

"I like that." His voice lowered, deep, gravelly and so erotically sexy it made her tremble more. "Come for me, Lana."

"S-soon, ohh."

"Now, Lana. I want to feel your tightness hold me, squeeze me."

She could hear the strain in his voice and knew he was about to come with her. His words excited her, carrying her higher and faster. She did as he commanded, let herself go, let the sweet sensations build low in her belly and explode to the very tips of her fingers and toes until she fell apart in his arms.

She let out a cry, and all her breath whooshed out of her lungs. She hung there in his arms, buffered by the water. Grant continued to drive into her, his groans rising, his pace increasing and his fingers never letting up on her clit until she thought she would lose consciousness. Another blinding and even more powerful orgasm shuddered through her—just as he gave one last plunge and held himself deep within her, his face now buried in her neck as he let out his roar of release.

Slowly the sound of the blood rushing in her ears calmed, and her breathing slowed. Grant also regained his composure, but never let go of her. They floated quietly in the warm water.

8

LANA WAS IN sensory overload. Since arriving in Hawaii three days ago, Grant had whisked her just about everywhere. Not only was the sex amazing, they seemed to have a great rapport. Grant was almost too good to be true. She couldn't help but worry that if something seemed too good to be true, it usually was.

"Stop it, Lana," she reprimanded herself out loud as she ran her fingers along the spines of the books on the shelf. Even though she was exhausted after their night of sweet love and the sunrise helicopter ride back to Honolulu, she couldn't sleep.

After arriving back at his beach house, Grant had quickly gotten ready, then kissed her passionately at the door before zooming off—in another amazing car—to take care of business. He'd be gone for a good part of the day and had told Lana to make herself at home.

She had her own important meeting with her boss next week. Maybe she should be preparing for it, at least a little bit.

She turned her attention back to the books. He had a lot of classics on the shelf, but nothing she'd be able to get all the way through in one afternoon. So she grabbed a couple of picture books about Hawaii. The experience at the luau made her hungry for more.

Taking her finds out onto the lanai where they'd shared their first breakfast, Lana flipped through the coffee-table style book and ran her hand over its cover—a beautiful photograph, not the typical beach scene, but stunning green peaks rising from blue ocean. Opening the book, she scanned the inside to see where the picture had been taken. The North Shore of Kauai. Eager to see more she flipped over more pages, oohing and aahing over the spectacular scenery on each page.

Turning to a double-page image of lava flowing into the ocean, Lana found some loose photographs that had been tucked between the pages. Pushing the book aside she placed the photos in a pile before her.

She looked at the top one and her heart pounded. Grant and a stunning redhead looked back at her. She swallowed, feeling a little bit ill and slid that picture aside to see the next one. Her lips thinned. Grant had his arm around the woman's shoulders. He was pressing a kiss to her temple while she stared back at the camera, her palm resting on his bare chest. Lana's eyes were drawn to the woman's ring. A huge diamond, bigger than any she'd ever seen. Quickly she flipped through the rest of the photos. The majority of them were of Grant with this woman, plus a few of a crowd gathered around a low table at a luau.

Lana swallowed the bile that rose in her throat when she realized what she was looking at. Grant had a wife. He was married. Oh, God, what if he had children? The group was at the same luau he had taken her to last night. She jumped to her feet, the chair behind her flipping over, crashing on the tiled floor. How could he have lied?

Angry tears welled up in her eyes. She walked to the edge of the lanai and grabbed the railing, her knuckles turning white. She felt such a fool! Her mind raced, and for the first time the view did not thrill her. What was she going to do now?

He'd lied to her, betrayed her—used her. Lana calmed her breathing down, trying to remind herself she'd had a good time with him and they'd made no promises to each other. Still, she couldn't help the feeling of anguish. Quickly going back to the table she righted the chair, gathered up the pictures, shoved them in the book and put it back in its place on the shelf.

She had to leave. Get out. There was no way she could spend the day here in his house—the house he must share with his wife. She shuddered to think that she'd slept in the other woman's bed. Showered in her bathroom. Likely used all her soaps and stuff, too.

The need to flee overcame her. But how? She had no car, had left all of her credit cards and money in her hotel room. She swore at herself for being so stupid. Then she remembered—she always carried a little extra cash with her. Mad money, her mother had called it. Grabbing her purse she looked through all the pockets to make sure she'd stashed some away.

"Aha!" She pulled out some Canadian money from a secret pocket. "Better than nothing. I can exchange it at the hotel to pay for the cab," Lana muttered, feeling quite pleased with herself as she sent a silent thank-you to her mother.

Two hours later she was back in her hotel room,

alone. Thank God she hadn't listened to Grant when he'd asked her to check out of her room.

Opening her laptop Lana decided there was no time like the present to check email. It would be a welcome distraction, too. She barely registered any of the ones she scanned through. She forced her mind away from Grant and focused on her messages. One from her boss marked as urgent caught her eye.

"Oh, for God's sake! Are you kidding me?" Lana shouted. "I can't believe this. Men are just too stupid to live." She stood and paced back and forth, rubbing her forehead. He was coming in early and wanted to meet for dinner, on the…what did it say in the email? Seventeenth. What day was it today? She looked at the bottom of screen for the date. Today! And a client meeting tomorrow. She sucked in a calming breath. She had to get a grip and not let her anger at Grant or her boss get in the way.

But she *was* angry, plain and simple. How could Martin push up the meeting by a week and expect her to be ready in less than a day? He knew she was taking some vacation time.

She had a whole lot of damage control to do right now and she needed to put all the fun and frivolity of the last few days with Grant firmly aside. *But I loved every second of the days I've had.*

"Holy shit, now I'm screwed," she whispered to the empty room and pulled the files from her briefcase, spreading them out over the table. Lana closed the curtains so she wouldn't be distracted by the gorgeous view outside or the reminder that Grant was out there somewhere. Lana picked up the phone by her bed and called down to the front desk, telling them to hold all calls and making a special note that she wanted no visitors. She plugged her cell phone in to charge it but turned off its ringer.

She had worked too hard to be blown off course by a man. She'd gotten carried away with Grant, and look how that turned out. He was married, after all.

Taking a big breath, Lana organized everything on her table into neat piles, opened her presentation on her laptop and stared at the screen. The image of Grant's handsome face filled her vision. Hot tears pricked at her eyes and slipped down her cheeks. She let herself have only the briefest moment of pain, heartache touched with a tiny bit of nostalgia, before firmly pushing him out of her thoughts. They'd never be together again. She buried the memories deep and wiped away the tears.

She decided to order up a mountain of food from room service, a big pot of coffee—would it be the same coffee Grant had served her? She changed her mind and switched to hot chocolate. She'd need the sustenance anyway, and eating her way through this melodrama would be the only way to survive pulling an all-nighter with Martin to prepare for the client meeting.

It never failed to amazed her how quickly things could change.

THE HOUSE WAS dark when Grant roared up in the Porsche. The meeting about the North American expansion had gone on far too long. And now the meeting with Martin had been switched to tomorrow. It allayed his concern that Lana worked for Martin. She'd have mentioned it if her own meeting next week had been moved.

Taking the front steps by twos, Grant was surprised

the front door was unlocked. He'd told Lana to lock it after he left. Inside he cocked his head to listen for her. Quiet. He smiled. Was she waiting for him in the bedroom, ready to pounce? He crept down the hall. Perhaps he could surprise her, instead. In the darkened bedroom he could see the bed was made. He furrowed his brows and turned around. Maybe she was down at the gazebo.

All the exterior doors to the lanai were locked. There was no way she could get down there, except through these doors. Growing alarmed, Grant quickly searched the rest of the house. Pulling out his phone he called the hotel.

"Connect me to Lana Hunter's room, please."

"I'm sorry, sir. Ms. Hunter is not taking any calls."

What the hell?

"Please, can you just call up and let her know I'm on the phone?"

"I'm sorry sir, but no, she left specific instructions not to be disturbed."

Grant hung up. At least he knew where she was. Relief flooded through him, but he was baffled by the fact that she had left without a word. And now she wasn't taking any calls. He wandered back to the great room and opened the doors to the lanai. The frangipani-scented night air blew in, reminding him of last night when Lana'd had the flowers in her hair.

He pulled out his phone, about to call her, and realized he'd never gotten her cell phone number. He'd given her his card so it was up to her to call him now. He thought about going over to the hotel, but shook his head, decision made. Clearly she wanted to be alone, and he wasn't about to go chasing, even if every muscle in his body twitched to jump back in his car and take off down the highway to her.

If she wasn't taking calls, she must have a good reason for it and he'd respect her privacy. The most simple explanation was that something had come up with her job. But it did aggravate him that she'd gone without a word. The least she could have done was leave a note.

Plus, they'd made plans go to dinner tonight. He checked his watch. Another hour before their reservation. He stared out over dark water, a weight in his chest. Why did he get the feeling she wasn't going to show?

9

DINNER LAST NIGHT had been excruciating. Martin had torn a strip off her, gone up one side of her and down the other about the state of her report, not replying to his messages quickly enough and she'd just sat there and let him. He'd never been a very understanding guy. All business and no-nonsense. She'd given up trying to lighten the mood and crawled back inside herself until the dinner was finally over, escaping the minute she was able.

What kind of life did he have? She'd never looked at him as anything other than a square-headed, tough boss who pushed his employees until they found a new level of performance. And annoyance.

The fight had gone out of her. Emotionally drained from the dinner and up all night fixing the debacle of her report she'd caught hell over for today's meeting. She was exhausted. And now the client meeting had been moved to today. Martin hadn't mentioned the client's name and she was too brain-fried to think of asking, which she should have. Why was he keeping the client such a secret? This didn't make her job any easier. Could it get any worse?

She needed a couple of hours' sleep before her breakfast meeting with Martin at ten. Lana went out onto the balcony and breathed in the tropical pre-dawn air. Waikiki was still asleep. It was dark, but the sunrise was starting to lighten the horizon. It reminded her of yesterday's helicopter ride with Grant. So much had happened in just twenty-four hours that it felt like a dream.

Part of her felt a little bad she hadn't left a note or called to cancel the dinner plans with Grant. She'd totally forgotten about the dinner, her boss had had her so discombobulated. Lana wondered if Grant had gone anyway, and how long he might have sat there waiting for her. She pursed her lips, thinking about him at a table all alone. No, she wouldn't feel sorry for him. After all, he hadn't been truthful to her about his wife.

Lana turned her back on the rising sun and drew the blackout drapes. She needed sleep for the hellish day ahead.

THE MORNING HAD gone by fine, if stressfully. But that was par for the course with Martin. They'd worked straight through and she was only now able to escape for a bit to find lunch. She and Martin still had a jam-packed afternoon before the dinner.

The expansion of coffeehouses into Canada needed lots of fine tuning. She was going to propose a name change from the one Martin liked, King'ha. After some research, she'd come up with a couple of other names that she would present to the owner and CEO at dinner later. Kahiko, which in Hawaiian meant ancient, was easy to pronounce and lent an exotic flavor, or Honu, which meant turtle. Honu sounded a little more "Hawaiian" to her ears—and she loved sea turtles, too.

She frowned, since turtles reminded her of the first night she'd spent with Grant. He'd spoken of the sea turtles in the pool by the beach where an ancient king had kept a bunch stashed for whenever he had a taste for them. And the coffee project only succeeded in reminding her of the morning after their night of sweet love.

Lana didn't want to think of Grant now. She'd managed the whole day and most of last evening to keep him out of her thoughts and now all it took was the thought of a turtle to have him crashing back into them.

She wandered through the hotel, a bottle of water in one hand and a pastry in the other. Epic fail, because even that reminded her of the bakery Grant had taken her to. She had to shake him off. Maybe some sand between her toes would do the trick. She made her way toward the Banyan Courtyard.

On the veranda, Lana paused, inhaling and loving all the different smells. Everything from flowers to food to coconut-scented suntan lotion wafted on the breeze. She raised her face and closed her eyes, allowing herself to get lost in the pleasant sensation, doing her best to not let sultry memories of her time with Grant invade the peaceful moment.

He'd gotten under her skin a lot more than she'd first thought. Sighing, she walked down the steps toward the pool. Not really dressed for a stroll on the beach in her knee-length pencil skirt and three-quarter-length sleeved blouse, Lana toed off her shoes and kicked them under a chair before weaving her way between the sunbathers.

It was a bit cloudy today, the sun peeping out now

and then with a hint of rain in the air. It kind of made her feel better and matched her mood. She wasn't missing any of the glorious Hawaiian sun being cooped up all day and night when she should have been enjoying the rest of her vacation that Martin has intruded upon. It was still hot, though, and she undid the top buttons on her blouse, pulling it apart to let the breeze flow in.

She stood at the edge of the surf waiting for the waves to crawl up the beach and splash over her feet. Even the water was warm, but it was refreshing. She finished off her pastry, not really wanting to go back inside. Standing for a few more minutes she gazed out over the turquoise waters of Waikiki Bay. Her phone buzzed, and she quickly pulled it from her bra. A flash of disappointment swept through her when she saw it wasn't Grant. Only micromanaging Martin.

She shook her head and cursed under her breath. "Can I not even have a few minutes to myself?" She nearly pitched the phone into the waves.

Not for the first time Lana wondered if she should start looking for another position. When she got back to Toronto she'd list herself on an executive search engine. Tonight she would change her LinkedIn profile to reflect that she was interested in new opportunities. The phone buzzed again.

"Yeah, yeah, yeah, I'm coming," she told it and turned off the ringer. Back to the grind. She took her time, dragging her feet in the sand and walking back up to the pool—taking the long way—before fishing her shoes out from under the chair. She put her game face on and made her way to Martin's penthouse suite, which was doubling as their meeting room.

Strolling through the gracious lobby to the elevator,

Lana glanced at the chair Grant had been sitting in that night when he came to pick her up. It seemed a lifetime ago, not just a few days. Her heart clenched, and finally she admitted it to herself—she missed him. For the first time since she took off yesterday, she wondered if she might have jumped to conclusions and misunderstood the photos.

As she rode up to the penthouse, Lana decided she would give Grant a call tonight. He'd shown her such a good time—she needed to be more gracious.

"OKAY, THEN, LOOKS like we're good," Martin announced. He stood, walked over to the bar by the window and poured himself a drink of water. Lana watched him, relieved their marathon of number crunching and strategic planning was done.

"Then I think I'm going to go to my room for a bit." Lana piled all the papers neatly.

"Why?" Martin asked. "You need to be here for the next meeting."

Lana let out a frustrated sigh. Martin gave her a surprised look and quite frankly she didn't care. "Because I've been stuck in this room all day and in my hotel room most of yesterday and last night. I need a moment to myself."

"You had a break at lunch." He turned his back on her and gazed out the window, then looked at his watch. "He should be arriving any time." There was a knock at the door the moment as he finished speaking and Martin shot her a superior smile. "Right on time." Martin greeted the businessman at the door. "Mr. Rankin, it's a pleasure to meet you."

Rankin? Lana sat up a little taller. *Why did that name*

sound familiar? The sound of footsteps approached and in that moment she remembered a business card given to her on a plane a couple of days ago. Was it really Grant?

Lana swiveled in the seat, and when the men entered the room she stood up with a sharp intake of breath. "This is Ms. Hunter." Little did he know that she knew *Mr. Rankin* a hell of a lot better than Martin would ever imagine.

Lana met Grant's gaze. Had she seen a flash of surprise, pleasure, before it shuttered to an unreadable expression? She saw a muscle work in his jaw, a new set to his lips she hadn't seen before and a pinched expression at the edge of his eyes.

She'd never seen him angry or upset, and if she had to guess, this was it. She clasped her hands behind her back and shifted uncomfortably from one foot to the next, suddenly feeling very exposed.

"Lana! Don't just stand there and be rude," Martin barked.

"It's quite okay." Grant interjected and stepped toward her. His hand was out and she dropped her gaze to it, remembering all the delights he and that hand had given her. No matter how hard she might try to forget, Lana knew he would always be the best lover she'd ever had. And the one that she had run from.

But now wasn't the time to get lost in sensual thoughts. He was a client, paying their company a lot of money to do their due diligence.

"Ms. Hunter." His voice was monotone. She glanced up into his face, but she couldn't see any emotion there.

When his fingers closed over hers she nearly melted into a puddle at the charge that crackled between them, and she tried desperately to keep her voice even. "Mr. Rankin."

Grant tightened his hold on her so she couldn't pull her hand from his grip. Her gaze was locked with his, and her heart tumbled when she saw a fleeting expression of pain behind his chocolaty eyes.

She'd hurt him.

Martin moved behind Grant, and her attention was drawn to him. He was looking at her with a stern expression and sharply nodding his head to her seat. She still couldn't pull her hand from Grant's and was relieved when Martin spoke.

"Now, then, shall we get down to business? The sooner we can wrap this up, the sooner we can head to dinner. I've had a table reserved on the veranda so we can take in the sunset over a fine meal."

Rather than letting her go, Grant guided her to the table and pulled out a chair for her with his free hand. As she moved to seat herself she froze—Grant's fingers touched her back and swept up her spine as she plopped very ungracefully into the chair. She shivered when he stroked up her neck and tried to keep herself from panting. Why was he torturing her so? Glancing under her brows at Martin, hoping he hadn't noticed, she was relieved to see he was standing at the bar pouring water for them all.

"Stop," Lana whispered, switching her gaze up to Grant, who stood unbearably close to her.

But he didn't do as she asked and stroked her neck lightly before trailing his fingers down her shoulder.

"You never complained before." His expression was still unreadable, but the pinched look around his eyes seemed to be softening.

Martin turned to them and Grant took the chair next to her, leaning back as if he didn't have a care in the world. His muscular legs, encased in very well-made trousers, spread wide. She did a double take, noticing the pleasant bulge in his pants, which only made her blood rush hotter through her veins.

She forced herself to look away, only to find herself gawking at his arms crossed over his massive chest. She needed a cool drink of water to dampen the fire he'd just ignited inside her. Lana scrambled for one of the glasses Martin had just placed on the table, but as she reached for it, the press of Grant's solid thigh against hers nearly had her catapulting out of her chair. She knocked the cut crystal glass, spilling water over the table.

"Oh, no!" she blurted. She quickly grabbed the glass, trying to set it right but only scattering droplets of water across the paperwork and making the glass roll crazily.

"Lana, for God's sake, stop." Martin lurched up, grabbing the papers to safety. "Please calm down and go get a towel."

She needed no further encouragement and fled to the bathroom, thankful for a moment to regain her composure. She shut the door behind her, put her hands on her head and sucked in a deep breath.

Get a grip, girl.

She looked in the mirror and patted her cheeks, trying to snap herself out of her sudden insecurity. She tucked her hair behind her ears, grabbed a towel and went out to take care of her mess.

One way or another, she had to face Grant without making a complete fool of herself.

10

"SILLY GIRL," MARTIN MUTTERED as Lana dashed to the bathroom.

Grant had a rash of confusing emotions when he saw Lana standing across the room, against the backdrop of the beautiful vista outside the penthouse's large windows. His heart had lurched painfully in his chest, and it had taken all his willpower not to rush over to her, demand to know why she taken off. It was thoughtless of her and a new side he hadn't anticipated seeing in her. Not to mention her no-show at dinner last night. Yet here she was. In the flesh.

He'd play along and see where she would take this. If he had to pretend he didn't know her so her boss wouldn't suspect anything, then that would be fine. But it didn't mean he couldn't make her squirm along the way. He knew which buttons to press to trigger a response in her. The first one had been helping her to her seat and running his fingers up her spine, feeling her shiver. And hearing her soft sigh was music to his ears.

His cock thickened and his balls grew heavy, a reaction he hadn't really expected and that effectively foiled his plan of teasing her. Getting himself seated to hide his hard-on had become paramount. Then he'd pressed his leg to hers, the need to keep feeling her overpowering.

Before Martin could rant about Lana's clumsiness, Grant interrupted him. "No worries, it was just an accident and it's only water."

"It was carelessness. She's not been herself these last couple of days and I must apologize for her lack of professionalism."

Grant wasn't about to allow him to bash Lana, so he shut Martin down in a deep, firm voice. "I said, it's no problem." Martin stilled and looked at him, surprised. Clearly, he wasn't used to people challenging him.

So Lana "hadn't been herself" lately? Interesting.

"Right, well, she should be out momentarily." Martin didn't speak again until Lana returned with a towel.

"Here, Lana, give me that." Grant reached out for it.

"No, it's fine. I can do it."

Grant placed his fingers on her forearm, and gently took the towel from her. "Relax, it's okay." He cast a quick glance at Martin, as if to remind him to let it go.

"Th-thanks. I'm sorry."

Grant turned, his gaze connecting with Lana's. Her lower lip trembled, and suddenly he wanted to wrap his arms around her and make it all better.

"For what? It's only water." Grant smiled, hoping she'd ease up on herself.

"For everything." She gave him a steady look.

Yes, they needed to talk after this meeting. About a number of things.

LANA WAS DYING. Couldn't wait for this meeting to be over so she could talk to Grant alone. She fidgeted, causing Martin to send her stern-eyed glances every now and then, so she focused on the paperwork in front of her, aware of the steady press of Grant's thigh against hers.

She felt his energy, his sexuality radiating off him in heavy waves, wrapping around her in a teasing and erotic haze. More importantly, she felt something else. Something deeper, sweeter, and it filled her with wonder. Sure, she needed to explain her rapid departure yesterday, but he needed to explain a few things, too. Why hadn't he told her he was owner of this company? As she thought back over their time together, the comments about coffee became clues. He'd had any number of opportunities to tell her who he was. Why had he hidden it?

Then it dawned on her. The house on the big island, the coffee plantation—did he own those, too? Out of the corner of her eye she saw Martin give her another stare, which she ignored as she turned to look at Grant. She met his gaze. Her increasing clarity and understanding made her angry. He'd been lying to her all along. Just what was the truth about him? Grant's smile slowly turned to a frown and his brows furrowed, likely because Lana knew her feelings were showing. And she didn't care.

She'd been hobnobbing and having sex with a very wealthy and sound businessman, probably a married one. A man with lots of secrets and lies. Not just the little white kind, but big, impactful ones. Ones that reflected a personality of deception. The more she thought about the secrets, the less guilty she felt about leaving him so suddenly. She was pissed.

Lana moved her thigh from his and slid the chair

away a bit wanting—needing—to put space between them. He was still watching her, a frown curving his very kissable lips. Lana didn't break their gaze and fought to keep eye contact with him. *Stop thinking about kissing him. You're mad at him and he needs to know that.*

For the remainder of the meeting, Lana kept her focus on the job at hand, doing her best to ignore the distraction of Grant's closeness. Which made her frustrated in more ways than one.

After two hours, they'd covered everything on the agenda, including naming the coffeehouses. Grant had chosen her suggestion. Honu. He even approved of her sea turtle logo idea. She liked that.

He signed the contract, which meant the expansion was good to go. Lana felt no sense of satisfaction at a job well done, her emotions too caught up in all the upheaval.

"Perfect timing," Martin announced. "Shall we head down to dinner?"

They all rose, and Lana wondered if she could escape for a few minutes to collect her thoughts before having to spend another couple of hours with the two men. In the elevator she punched her floor number and then ground her teeth when Martin started to talk.

"Lana, are you not joining us for dinner?"

She turned to face him, giving him the sweetest smile she could muster up under the circumstances. But her voice was steel. "Yes, I'm just stopping by my room first. *If* that's okay with you."

The doors whooshed open and she stepped out before Martin could speak, commenting over her shoulder, "I'll be down shortly. Please don't wait for me to order."

She raced down the hall and took refuge in her room for as long as she thought she could get away with it. To hell with a proper skirt and blouse, she needed to breathe. She was in Hawaii and decided to play the part. Stripping off the no-nonsense business clothes, she threw them in the corner and changed into a colorful sarong shot with sparkly thread and tiny crystals. She matched it with a lightweight, formfitting black crocheted top with straps made of jet beads that caught the light. The neckline was low and sat nicely on the rise of her breasts. *Take that, Grant!*

Turning before the mirror to check her look, Lana was pleased with the result. Exotically sexy if she did say so herself. The hell with it if Martin disapproved. She didn't have any jewelry to accent it, but knew of a frangipani tree where she could pluck a flower for her hair. That ought to bring back a memory or two for Grant.

Who was she kidding? She might be mad at Grant, but she was still as attracted as hell to him. And maybe a part of her also wanted to twist the knife so he knew what he was going to be missing.

SHE SPOTTED THE men across the room and zeroed her gaze on Grant. Lifting her chin and straightening her shoulders, she made her way to the table in the corner. The view was nothing compared to Grant. He'd hung his suit jacket on the back of the chair and rolled up his sleeves, exposing his muscular forearms. She had the urge to run her fingertips over the fine hairs and closed her eyes quickly, not wanting to enjoy the burst of arousal in her belly.

No doubt about it, he was one sexy beast. With his

attention on Martin, she could watch him without his knowing. She let her gaze crawl over him, imprinting him in her mind. Then he turned and his dark eyes met hers. It almost made her pause in her step, but she forced herself to keep going. She smiled at him and though his eyebrows rose in surprise, he returned her smile. He stood as she got closer and pulled a chair out for her.

Boldly looking at her, his gaze raked over her body, down to her toes and then slowly back up to her face. Lana's heart beat quicker and suddenly she felt hot. From the inside out. She fought to keep herself calm, but her body betrayed her and excitement grew. She knew what it was like to be in this man's arms, and her body wanted it again.

"You look beautiful, Lana," Grant said in a low sultry voice.

She nodded and flicked her gaze up to him, not breaking eye contact as he settled into the chair beside her. She completely forgot Martin was across the table until he spoke.

"This calls for a celebration." Martin raised his hand and snapped his fingers. That entitled gesture cemented Lana's decision not to work for him any longer. He grated on her every nerve and she was no longer able to brush it aside. Having been in Grant's company and seeing him as she had, so kind and polite to all around him no matter how high powered or super rich he was only threw Martin into worse light. She couldn't be part of that any longer. The waiter approached and Martin took the wine list from him. "A bottle of Cristal will do nicely." He handed the wine list back to the waiter without a second glance. Lana smiled at the waiter, trying to make up for Martin's rudeness.

Lana got through dinner, but not without a whole lot of suffering, her distaste for Martin building along with her awareness of Grant beside her. Feeling his tension, which spiked her own. Her body warred with arousal, anger and confusion, and she was wound tighter than a drum.

The champagne began to take the edge off, and she gulped the remainder of her glass and turned to Grant. "We need to talk."

Grant leaned back in his chair, every move he made smooth and sensual, reaching right inside her like warm fingers grabbing her heart. "Do we now?" His voice held a touch of strain, reminding her of the times they made love.

She nodded and swallowed the lump forming in her throat.

Martin interrupted them. "Lana, I don't think the time is right. And what could you possibly have to talk about? This is a business dinner."

Lana turned her gaze on her boss. "Martin, I quit."

He sputtered, blinking rapidly, "B-but I don't accept your resignation. You're needed on this account—"

Lana shook her head. "No, I'm not. When I get back to Toronto I'll give you two weeks, a month if you need it, to replace me, but I'm moving on."

She stood, her eyes catching Grant's. His look of amusement made her smile for the first time since she'd walked out of his house yesterday. She held out her hand to him. "Are you coming?"

He nodded and stood, taking her hand.

"But, I don't understand…" Martin sputtered.

Lana felt a twinge of pity for him. She softened her tone and tried to explain, "Martin, working for you has been a great opportunity for me. But I need to move on and establish myself outside of your company. I'll help find a replacement, but as of now, I'm on holiday until I come back to Canada. I'll see you next week."

She turned and gently tugged Grant's hand. It was time to clear the air.

11

LANA COULDN'T GET Grant outside quickly enough. She dragged him through the hotel, down past the pool and out onto the sand. He didn't say a word the entire time.

Now that she had him where she wanted him, she stood frozen at the edge of the surf, her back to him, warm waves rushing up over her feet. She stared out across the sea, watching the distant twinkly lights on the catamarans as they bobbed up and down in the swells.

Her body began to tremble, and Grant stepped in close behind, his arms circling her waist as he had done so many times over the past few days. She sighed and leaned back in to him, loving how she fit so perfectly with his body. Even though everything felt so right with him, she needed to know. Get answers to her questions.

His breath next to her ear fluttered her hair and she tipped her head sideways, knowing he would find that supersensitive spot with his lips. He didn't let her down and she moaned. His hands splayed across her belly, holding her against him so she couldn't miss his arousal. His cock pressed against her bottom, making her melt.

She didn't pull away when his other hand crept up between her breasts and slid to cover one, gently kneading until she felt her nipples rise up, aching for his touch.

"G-Grant. Stop. Please," she whispered, unsure if he heard the words as the breeze off the water stole them from her lips. Pushing his hands away was almost impossible to do, but she had to. They did need to talk. She stepped out of the circle of his heat and turned around to face him. Rather than allowing her to speak he yanked her roughly against his chest, threaded his fingers in her hair and pulled her head back.

She could see everything in his eyes. Not just arousal, but more, and her lips parted, waiting for him. Knowing that this kiss would be the most important one they ever shared. And possibly the last.

As his mouth sealed over hers, she met his tongue with her own. She let herself get lost in him, just as a great explosion startled them both. Fireworks erupted in the night sky.

Grant leaned down and whispered in her ear, "I didn't need those fireworks to go off. You light me up all on your own."

Lana watched the display for a moment before turning back to Grant. "Are you married?"

He looked as if he'd just been punched in the gut and stepped away from her. "What are you talking about?"

"Answer me. Are. You. Married? Simple yes or no question."

He stared down at her for a few excruciating seconds before shaking his head. "No."

Relief flooded through her and she had to swallow back an almost hysterical giggle that bubbled up her throat. But she still needed to find out the whole truth. "When I saw you with that woman…"

"What woman?"

"Oh, come on. I found pictures of you! Next to a redhead with a big-ass diamond on her finger." She held up her left hand and wiggled her fingers, unable to contain the bitter tone that crept into her voice. "You looked blissfully happy."

Grant burst out laughing and this time it was Lana who was confused. "What's so funny? I don't think it's very funny at all." She poked him in the chest. "And what about you owning this coffee company, too, and that was your house we were at the other night on the Big Island, wasn't it?" She was on a roll now and the words spilled out of her. She had to get it all out before he had a chance to distract her again. "All the stuff about you that I never knew, or rather that you never told me—which you should've by the way—and, and I…find out—"

To her horror, tears sprang into her eyes. She sucked in a breath, about to continue when Grant took her by the shoulders and pulled her close, trapping her with his gaze. The look in his eyes melted her heart. A softness that had never been there before grew, as did his gentle smile and that damned dimple in his cheek, making him look so vulnerable and cute.

"Lana, calm yourself, ya. I don't know what pictures you're talking about, but I'm not married now. Haven't been for almost three years. The redhead is my ex-wife."

He's divorced. "Any kids?" she blurted.

He chuckled and shook his head. "No kids." He kissed her on the forehead and then looked deep into her eyes again. "We weren't married long, it was pretty much over before it started and should never have happened in the first place."

"Oh. But why didn't you tell me?"

"Because I don't think about that part of my life. It's over. It's not important."

"But…"

He sighed, but didn't look annoyed. "What else?"

"There were many opportunities for you to tell me you owned this coffee company. Why did you hide who you were?"

"Because we had just met and the fact that you didn't know anything about me was refreshing. I needed to know you liked me for me and not because I own the company or had these houses in Hawaii. Yes, the house on the Big Island is mine, too."

"Why?"

"In my experience, some women can be blinded by these things. I've already been through that and don't plan on doing it again."

Lana nodded, accepting his answers. "I understand. I want you to know I wasn't snooping in your house. I was just looking at some books on your shelf and the pictures fell out."

"I'm sorry you had to find them."

"When we were talking about coffee, when I mentioned my business…were you keeping things from me then, too?"

"At first I had a suspicion we could be coming in for the same meeting. Remember what you said to me on the plane?" He paused and looked at her expectantly.

Lana furrowed her brow and recalled their conversation, but couldn't pinpoint anything that would hold significance for him. "Tell me."

"Your feelings were very strong about business romance. So I didn't say anything at the time. But then it didn't seem like our meetings were connected so…" He shrugged and squeezed her shoulders, giving her a little shake. "Why did you run off? Why didn't you wait and ask me then, to save all this upset?"

"Well, I've been burned in the past, too. By lying and cheating men. It was easier just to go. I know now I should've waited or at least phoned you and asked you."

He pulled her tight and wrapped his arms around her. "Then we both learned a lesson, didn't we?"

Lana snuggled into him, emotion swelling within her.

"And I quit my job! Holy shit."

"Yes, you did. What do they say? When one door closes another one opens? I'll be needing someone to run the Canadian operations."

Lana looked up at him, shocked.

"Are you offering me a job?" she asked.

"Just that. You think you can handle it? I mean, would you be able to keep our personal and professional lives separate? And there will be travel involved. I will make sure of that."

Lana smiled. He was serious and this was the opportunity she had been waiting for, in her career and in her heart. But she felt like teasing him a little.

"Well, I don't know. Remember, I'm not a fan of office romance."

Grant burst out laughing.

"Hmm, then maybe we have to have a different plan, ya? I want you in my bedroom and in my boardroom. Lana, the days we spent together were the best I've ever experienced. I'm sorry you were hurt by me not telling you who I was, but I hope you understand." She nodded, never looking away from him. "When you left yesterday it was as if the light had gone out of my world. I don't ever want that to happen again."

"Oh, Grant, I was a wreck after I left! But when I got Martin's email that the meeting had been moved up I was angry at myself for being so swept away by you. Knowing it may have compromised my career." She laughed, and then said, "I had no idea I was going to quit, though."

He shushed her with a kiss and then murmured next to her lips, "Stay with me. I know you need your career, but I need you in my life. I never want to let you go."

Lana threw her arms around his neck. "Me either. I can't believe how much you've become a part of me in such a short time. We can make it work. Right?" She looked up at him, and his confident smile was all she needed.

"I'm sure of it."

Lana stepped away and gave him a sultry smile. She stretched out her hand. "Deal. We can work it out. But right now, I'm officially on holiday. How about you? Can you take a week or so off?"

Grant's laughter filled her heart with joy. His warm fingers closed around hers, sending a thrill up her arm that rushed right down to settle with liquid fire in her belly. Good God, this man had the touch and it seemed as if that touch was just for her now.

"No, we're not shaking on this." Grant's voice was tight as he pulled her to him. "This deal is being sealed with a kiss."

She threw back her head and laughed. Flinging her arms around his neck, she jumped up so he had to catch her. He silenced her with his lips, slanting them across hers. Lana opened to him in every sense—her heart, her trust, her future.

"Now, what do you say we clear out your room and go back to the grass shack. If you like, we can stay there or fly over to my other house. The choice is yours, my lovely."

*   *   *   *   *

If you like fun, sexy and steamy stories with strong heroines and irresistible heroes, you'll love THE HARDER YOU FALL by New York Times *bestselling author Gena Showalter—featuring Jessie Kay Dillon and Lincoln West, the sexy bachelor who's breaking all his rules for this rowdy Southern belle...*

Turn the page for a sneak peek at THE HARDER YOU FALL!

WEST HAD BROUGHT a date.

The realization hit Jessie Kay like a bolt of lightning in a freak storm. Great! Wonderful! While she'd opted not to bring Daniel, and thus make West the only single person present—and embarrassingly alone—he'd chosen his next two-month "relationship" and hung Jessie Kay out to dry.

Hidden in the back of the sanctuary, Jessie Kay stood in the doorway used by church personnel and scowled. Harlow had asked for—cough, banshee-screeched, cough—a status report. Jessie Kay had abandoned her precious curling iron in order to sneak a peek at the guys.

Now she pulled her phone out of the pocket in her dress to text Daniel. Oops. She'd missed a text.

Sunny: Party 2nite?????

She made a mental note to respond to Sunny later and drafted her note to Daniel.

I'm at the church. How fast can you get here? I need a friend/date for Harlow's wedding

A response didn't come right away. She knew he'd gone on a date last night and the girl had stayed the night with him. How did she know? Because he'd texted Jessie Kay to ask how early he could give the snoring girl the boot.

Sooo glad I never hooked up with him.

Finally, a vibration signaled a response.

Any other time I'd race to your rescue, even though weddings are snorefests. Today I'm in the city on a job

He'd started some kind of high-risk security firm with a few of his Army buddies.

Her: Fine. You suck. I clearly need to rethink our friendship

Daniel: I'll make it up to you, swear. Want to have dinner later???

She slid her phone back in place without responding, adding his name to her mental note. If he wasn't going to ignore his responsibilities whenever she had a minor need, he deserved to suffer for a little while.

Of its own accord, Jessie Kay's gaze returned to West. The past week, she'd seen him only twice. Both times, she'd gone to the farmhouse to help her sister with sandwiches and casseroles, and he'd taken one look at her, grabbed his keys and driven off.

Would it have killed him to acknowledge her presence by calling her by some hateful name, per usual? After all, he'd had the nerve to flirt with her at the diner, to look at her as if she'd stripped naked and begged him to have *her* for dessert. And now he ignored her? Men! This one in particular.

Her irritation grew as he introduced his date to Kenna Starr and her fiancé, Dane Michaelson. Kenna was a stunning redhead who'd always been Brook Lynn's partner in crime. The girl who'd done what Jessie Kay had not, saving her sister every time she'd gotten into trouble.

Next up was an introduction to Daphne Roberts, the mother of Jase's nine-year-old daughter, Hope, then Brad Lintz, Daphne's boyfriend.

Jase and Beck joined the happy group, but the brunette never looked away from West, as if he was speaking the good Lord's gospel. Her adoration was palpable.

A sharp pang had Jessie Kay clutching her chest. *Too young for a heart attack.*

Indigestion?

Yeah. Had to be.

The couple should have looked odd together. West was too tall and the brunette was far too short for him. A skyscraper next to a one-story house. But somehow, despite their height difference, the two actually complemented each other.

And really, the girl's adoration had to be good for West, buoying him the way Daniel's praise often buoyed Jessie Kay. Only on a much higher level, considering the girl was more than a friend to West.

Deep down, Jessie Kay was actually...happy for West. As crappy as his childhood had been, he deserved a nice slice of contentment.

Look at me, acting like a big girl and crap.

When West wrapped his arm around the brunette's waist, drawing her closer, Jessie Kay's nails dug into her palms.

I'm happy for him, remember? Besides, big girls didn't want to push other women in front of a speeding bus.

Jessie Kay's phone buzzed. Another text. This one from Brook Lynn.

Hurry! Bridezilla is on a rampage!!!

Her: Tell her the guys look amazing in their tuxes—no stains or tears yet—and the room is gorgeous. Or just tell her NOTHING HAS FREAKING CHANGED

The foster bros had gone all out even though the ceremony was to be a small and intimate affair. There were red and white roses at the corner of every pew, and in front of the pulpit was an ivory arch with wispy jewel-encrusted lace.

With a sigh, she added an adorable smiley face to her message, because it was cute and it said I'm not yelling at you. My temper is not engaged.

Send.

Brook Lynn: Harlow wants a play-by-play of the action

Fine.

Beck is now speaking w/Pastor Washington. Jase, Dane, Kenna, Daphne & Brad are engaged in conversation, while Hope is playing w/ her doll on the floor. Happy?

She didn't add that West was focused on the stunning brunette, who was still clinging to his side.

The girl…she had a familiar face—*where have I seen her?*—and a body so finely honed Jessie Kay wanted to stuff a few thousand Twinkies down her throat just to make it fair for the rest of the female population. Her designer dress was made of ebony silk and hugged her curves like a besotted lover.

Like West would be doing tonight?

Grinding her teeth, Jessie Kay slid her gaze over her own gown. One she'd sewn in her spare time. Not bad—actually kind of awesome—but compared to Great Bod's delicious apple it was a rotten orange.

A wave of jealousy swept over her. Dang it! Jealousy was stupid. Jessie Kay was no can of dog food in the looks department. In fact, she was well able to hold her own against anyone, anywhere, anytime. But…but…

A lot of baggage came with her.

West suddenly stiffened, as if he knew he was being watched. He turned. Her heart slamming against her ribs with enough force to break free and escape, she darted into Harlow's bridal chamber—the choir room.

Harlow finished curling her thick mass of hair as Brook Lynn gave her lips a final swipe of gloss.

"Welcome to my nightmare," Jessie Kay announced. "I might as well put in rollers, pull on a pair of mom jeans and buy ten thousand cats." Cats! Want! "I'm officially an old maid without any decent prospects."

Brook Lynn wrinkled her brow. "What are you talking about?"

"Everyone is here, including West and his date. I'm the only single person in our group, which means you guys have to set me up with your favorite guy friends. Obviously I'm looking for a nine or ten. Make it happen. Please and thank you."

Harlow went still. "West brought a date? Who is it?"

Had a curl of steam just risen from her nostrils? "Just some girl."

Harlow pressed her hands against a stomach that had to be dancing with nerves. "I don't want *just some girl* at my first wedding."

"You planning your divorce to Beck already?"

Harlow scowled at her. "Not funny. You know we're planning a larger ceremony next year."

Jessie Kay raised her hands, palms out. "You're right, you're right. And you totally convinced me. I'll kick the bitch out pronto." *And I'll love every second of it—on Harlow's behalf.*

"No. No. I don't want a scene." Stomping her foot, Harlow added, "What was West thinking? He's ruined *everything.*"

Ooo-kay. A wee bit dramatic, maybe. "I doubt he was thinking at all. If that boy ever had an idea, it surely died of loneliness." Too much? "Anyway. I'm sure you could use a glass or six of champagne. I'll open the bottle for us—for you. You're welcome."

A wrist corsage hit her square in the chest.

"This is *my* day, Jessica Dillon." Harlow thumped her chest. "Mine! You will remain stone-cold sober, or I will remove your head, place it on a stick and wave it around while your sister sobs over your bleeding corpse."

Wow. "That's pretty specific, but I feel you. No alcohol for me, ma'am." She gave a jaunty salute. "I mean, no alcohol for me, Miss Bridezilla, sir."

"Ha-ha." Harlow morphed from fire-breathing dragon to fairy-tale princess in an instant, twirling in a circle. "Now stop messing around and tell me how amazing I look. And don't hesitate to use words like *exquisite* and *magical.*"

The hair at her temples had been pulled back, but the rest hung to her elbows in waves so dark they glimmered blue in the light. The gown had capped sleeves and a straight bustline with a cinched-in waist and pleats that flowed all the way to the floor, covering the sensible flats she'd chosen based on West's advice. "You look…exquisitely magical."

"Magically exquisite," Brook Lynn said with a nod.

"My scars aren't hideous?" Self-conscious, Harlow smoothed a hand over the multitude of jagged pink lines running between her breasts, courtesy of an attack she'd miraculously survived as a teenage girl.

"Are you kidding? Those scars make you look badass." Jessie Kay curled a few more pieces of hair, adding, "I'm bummed my skin is so flawless."

Harlow snorted. "Yes, let's shed a tear for you."

Jessie Kay gave her sister the stink eye. "You better not be like this for your wedding. I won't survive two of you."

Brook Lynn held up her well-manicured hands, all innocence.

"Well." She glanced at a wristwatch she wasn't wearing, doing her best impression of West. "We've got twenty minutes before the festivities kick off. Need anything?"

Harlow's hands returned to her stomach, the color draining from her cheeks in a hurry. "Yes. Beck."

Blinking, certain she'd misheard, she fired off a quick "Excuse me?" Heck. Deck. Neck. Certainly not Beck. "Grooms aren't supposed to see—"

"I need Beck." Harlow stomped her foot. *"Now."*

"Have you changed your mind?" Brook Lynn asked. "If so, we'll—"

"No, no. Nothing like that." Harlow launched into a quick pace, marching back and forth through the room. "I just… I need to see him. He hates change, and this is the biggest one of all, and I need to talk to him before I totally. Flip. Out. Okay? All right?"

"This isn't that big a change, honey. Not really." Who would have guessed Jessie Kay would be a voice of reason in a situation like this. Or *any* situation? "You guys live together already."

"Beck!" she insisted. "Beck, Beck, Beck."

"Temper tantrums are not attractive." Jessie Kay shared a concerned look with her sister, who nodded. "All right. One Beck coming up." As fast as her heels would allow, she made her way back to the sanctuary.

She purposely avoided West's general direction, focusing only on the groom. "Harlow has decided to throw millions of years' worth of tradition out the window. She wants to see you without delay. Are you wearing a cup? I'd wear a cup. Good luck."

He'd been in the middle of a conversation with Jase, and like Harlow, he quickly paled. "Is something wrong with her?" He didn't stick around for an answer, rushing past Jessie Kay without actually judging the distance between them, almost knocking her over.

As she stumbled, West flew over and latched on to her wrist to help steady her. The contact nearly buckled her knees. His hands were calloused, his fingers firm. His strength unparalleled and his skin hot enough to burn. Electric tingles rushed through her, the world around her fading from existence until they were the only two people in existence.

Fighting for every breath, she stared up at him. His

gaze dropped to her lips and narrowed, his focus savagely carnal and primal in its possessiveness, as if he saw nothing else, either—wanted nothing and no one else ever. But as he slowly lowered his arm and stepped away from her, the world snapped back into motion.

The bastard brought a date.

Right. She cleared her throat, embarrassed by the force of her reaction to him. "Thanks."

A muscle jumped in his jaw. A sign of anger? "May I speak with you privately?"

Uh… "Why?"

"Please."

What the what now? Had Lincoln West actually said the word *please* to her? *Her?* "Whatever you have to say to me—" an insult, no doubt "—can wait. You should return to your flavor of the year." Opting for honesty, she grudgingly added, "You guys look good together."

The muscle jumped again, harder, faster. "You think we look good together?"

"Very much so." Two perfect people. "I'm not being sarcastic, if that's what you're getting at. Who is she?"

"Monica Gentry. Fitness guru based in the city."

Well. That explained the sense of familiarity. And the body. Jessie Kay had once briefly considered thinking about exercising along with Monica's video. Then she'd found a bag of KIT KAT Minis and the insane idea went back to hell, where it belonged. "She's a good choice for you. Beautiful. Successful. Driven. And despite what you think about me, despite the animosity between us, I want you happy."

And not just because of his crappy childhood, she realized. He was a part of her family, for better or worse. A girl made exceptions for family. Even the douche bags.

His eyes narrowed to tiny slits. "We're going to speak privately, Jessie Kay, whether you agree or not. The only decision you need to make is whether or not you'll walk. I'm more than willing to carry you."

A girl also had the right to smack family. "You're just going to tell me to change my hideous dress, and I'm going to tell you I'm fixing to cancel your birth certificate."

When Harlow had proclaimed *Wear whatever you want*, Jessie Kay had done just that, creating a bloodred, off-the-shoulder, pencil-skirt dress that molded to her curves like a second skin…made from leftover material for drapes.

Scarlett O'Hara has nothing on me!

Jessie Kay was proud of her work, but she wasn't blind to its flaws. Knotted threads in the seams. Years had passed since she'd sewn anything, and her skills were rusty.

West gave her another once—twice—over as fire smoldered in his eyes. "Why would I tell you to change?" His voice dipped, nothing but smoke and gravel. "You and that dress are a fantasy come true."

Uh, what the what now? Had Lincoln West just called her *a fantasy*?

Almost can't process…

"Maybe you should take me to the ER, West. I think I just had a brain aneurysm." She rubbed her temples. "I'm hallucinating."

"Such a funny girl." He ran his tongue over his teeth, snatched her hand and while Monica called his name, dragged Jessie Kay to a small room in back. A cleaning closet, the air sharp with antiseptic. What little space was available was consumed by overstuffed shelves.

"When did you decide to switch careers and become a caveman?" she asked.

"When you decided to switch careers and become a femme fatale."

Have mercy on my soul.

He released her to run his fingers through his hair, leaving the strands in sexy spikes around his head. "Listen. I owe you an apology for the way I've treated you in the past. The way I've acted today. I shouldn't have manhandled you, and I'm very sorry."

Her eyes widened. Seriously, what the heck had happened to this man? In five minutes, he'd upended everything she'd come to expect from him.

And he wasn't done! "I'm sorry for every hurtful thing I've ever said to you. I'm sorry for making you feel bad about who you are and what you've done. I'm sorry—"

"Stop. Just stop." She placed her hands over her ears in case he failed to heed her order. "I don't understand what's happening."

He gently removed her hands and held on tight to her wrists. "What's happening? I'm owning my mistakes and hoping you're in a forgiving mood."

"You want to be my friend?" The words squeaked from her.

"I...do."

Why the hesitation? "Here's the problem. You're a dog and I'm a cat, and we're never going to get along."

One corner of his mouth quirked with lazy amusement, causing a flutter to skitter through her pulse. "I think you're wrong…kitten."

Kitten. A freakishly adorable nickname, and absolutely perfect for her. But also absolutely unexpected.

Oh, she'd known he'd give her one sooner or later. He and his friends enjoyed renaming the women in their lives. Jase always called Brook Lynn "angel" and Beck called Harlow everything from "beauty" to "hag," her initials. Well, HAG prewedding. But Jessie Kay had prepared herself for "demoness" or the always classic "bitch."

"Dogs and cats can be friends," he said, "especially when the dog minds his manners. I promise you, things will be different from now on."

"Well." Reeling, she could come up with no witty reply. "We could try, I guess."

"Good." His gaze dropped to her lips, heated a few more degrees. "Now all we have to do is decide what kind of friends we should be."

Her heart started kicking up a fuss all over again, breath abandoning her lungs. "What do you mean?"

"Text frequently? Call each other occasionally? Only speak when we're with our other friends?" He backed her into a shelf and cans rattled, threatening to fall. "Or should we be friends with benefits?"

The tingles returned, sweeping over her skin and sinking deep, deep into bone. Her entire body ached with sudden need and it was so powerful it nearly felled her. How long since a man had focused the full scope of his masculinity on her? Too long and never like this. Somehow West had reduced her to a quivering mess of femininity and whoremones.

"I vote…we only speak when we're with our other

friends," she said, embarrassed by the breathless tremor in her voice.

"What if I want all of it?" He placed his hands at her temples and several of the cans rolled to the floor. "The texts, the calls…and the benefits."

"No?" A question? Really? "No to the last. You have a date."

He scowled at her as if *she'd* done something wrong. "See, that's the real problem, kitten. I don't want her. I want you."

WEST CALLED HIMSELF a thousand kinds of fool. He'd planned to apologize, return to the sanctuary, witness his friend's wedding and start the countdown with Monica. The moment he'd gotten Jessie Kay inside the closet, her pecans-and-cinnamon scent in his nose, those plans burned to ash. Only one thing mattered.

Getting his hands on her.

From day one, she'd been a vertical g-force too strong to deny, pulling, pulling, *pulling* him into a bottomless vortex. He'd fought it every minute of every day since meeting her, and he'd gotten nowhere fast. Why not give in? Stop the madness?

Just once…

"We've been dancing around this for months," he said. "I'm scum for picking here and now to hash this out with you, and I'll care tomorrow. Right now, I think it's time we did something about our feelings."

"I don't…" She began to soften against him, only to snap to attention. "No. Absolutely not. I can't."

"You *won't*." *But I can change your mind…*

She nibbled on her bottom lip.

Something he would kill to do. So he did it. He leaned into her, caught her bottom lip between his teeth and ran the plump morsel through. "Do you want me, Jessie Kay?"

Her eyes closed for a moment, a shiver rocking her. "You say you'll care tomorrow, so I'll give you an answer then. As for today, I... I... I'm leaving." But she made no effort to move away, and he knew. She did want him. As badly as he wanted her. "Yes. Leaving. Any moment now..."

Acting without thought—purely on instinct—he placed his hands on her waist and pressed her against the hard line of his body. "I want you to stay. I want you, period."

"West." The new tremor in her voice injected his every masculine instinct with adrenaline, jacking him up. "You said it yourself. You're scum. This is wrong."

Anticipation raced denial to the tip of his tongue, and won by a photo finish. "Do you care?" He caressed his way to her ass and cupped the perfect globes, then urged her forward to rub her against the long length of his erection. The woman who'd tormented his days and invaded his dreams moaned a decadent sound of satisfaction and it did something to him. Made his need for her *worse*.

She wasn't what he should want, but somehow she'd become everything he could not resist, and he was tired, so damn tired, of walking, hell, running away from her.

"Do you?" he insisted. "Say yes, and *I'll* be the one to leave. I don't want you to regret this." He wanted her desperate for more.

She looked away from him, licked her lips. "Right at this moment? No. I don't care." As soft as a whisper.

Triumph filled him, his clasp on her tightening.

"But tomorrow..." she added.

Yes. Tomorrow. He wasn't the only one who'd been running from the sizzle between them, but today, with her admission ringing in his ears, he wasn't letting her get away. One look at her, that's all it had taken to ruin his plans. Now she would pay the price. Now she would make everything better.

"I *will* regret it," she said. "This is a mistake I've made too many times in the past."

Different emotions played over her features. Features so delicate he was consumed by the need to protect her from anything and anyone…but himself.

He saw misery, desire, fear, regret, hope and anger. The anger concerned him. This Southern belle could knock a man's testicles into his throat with a single swipe of her knee. Even still, West didn't walk away.

"For all we know, the world will end tomorrow. Let's focus on today. You tell me what you want me to do," he said, nuzzling his nose against her cheek, "and I'll do it."

More tremors rocked her. She traced her delicate hands up his tie and gave the knot a little shake, an action that was sexy, sweet and wicked all at once. "I want you…to go back to your date. You and I, we'll be friends as agreed, and we'll pretend this never happened." She pushed him, but he didn't budge.

His date. Yeah, he'd forgotten about Monica before Jessie Kay had mentioned her a few minutes ago. But then, he'd gotten used to forgetting everything whenever the luscious blonde entered a room. Everything about her consumed every part of him, and it was more than irritating, it was a sickness to be cured, an obstacle to be overcome and an addiction to be avoided. If they did this, he would suffer from his own regrets, but there was no question he would love the ride.

He bunched up the hem of her skirt, his fingers brushing the silken heat of her bare thigh. Her breath hitched, driving him wild. "You've told me what you *think* you should want me to do." He rasped the words against her mouth, hovering over her, not touching her but teasing with what could be. "Now tell me what you really want me to do."

Navy blues peered up at him, beseeching; the fight drained out of her, leaving only need and raw vulnerability. "I'm only using you for sex—said no guy ever. But that's what you're going to do. Isn't it? You're going to use me and lose me, just like the others."

Her features were utterly *ravaged*, and in that moment, he hated himself. Because she was right. Whether he took her for a single night or every night for two months, the end result would be the same. No matter how much it hurt her—no matter how much it hurt *him*—he would walk away.

Don't miss a single story in
THE ORIGINAL HEARTBREAKERS *series:*
"THE ONE YOU WANT" (novella)
THE CLOSER YOU COME
THE HOTTER YOU BURN
THE HARDER YOU FALL

*Available now from Gena Showalter
and HQN Books!*

Copyright © 2015 by Gena Showalter

COMING NEXT MONTH FROM

HARLEQUIN *Blaze*

Available December 15, 2015

#875 PLEASING HER SEAL
Uniformly Hot!
by Anne Marsh
Wedding blogger Madeline Holmes lives and breathes romance—from the sidelines. That is, until Navy SEAL Mason Black promises to fulfill all of her fantasies at an exclusive island resort. But is Mason her ultimate fantasy—could he be "the one"?

#876 RED HOT
Hotshot Heroes
by Lisa Childs
Forest ranger firefighter Wyatt Andrews battles the flames to keep others safe, but who will protect *him* from the fiery redhead who thinks he's endangering her little brother?

#877 HER SEXY VEGAS COWBOY
by Ali Olson
Jessica Gainey decides to take a wild ride with rancher Aaron Weathers while she's in Vegas. But when it's time to go home, how can she put those hot nights—and her sexy cowboy—behind her?

#878 PLAYING TO WIN
by Taryn Leigh Taylor
Reporter Holly Evans is determined to uncover star hockey captain Luke Maguire's sinful secrets. But when *he's* the one who turns the heat up on *her*, their sexy game is on...

YOU CAN FIND MORE INFORMATION ON UPCOMING HARLEQUIN® TITLES, FREE EXCERPTS AND MORE AT WWW.HARLEQUIN.COM.

HBCNM1215

EXCLUSIVE
Limited time offer!

$1.⁰⁰ OFF

New York Times bestselling author
GENA SHOWALTER
is back with another sizzling
Original Heartbreakers story featuring
an aloof bad boy and the rowdy
Southern belle who rocks his world...

THE *Harder* YOU FALL

Available November 24, 2015.
Pick up your copy today!

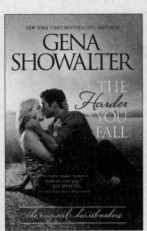

NEW YORK TIMES BESTSELLING AUTHOR
GENA SHOWALTER
THE *Harder* YOU FALL
the original heartbreakers

$7.99 U.S./$9.99 CAN.

H HQN™

$1.⁰⁰ OFF
the purchase price of
THE HARDER YOU FALL by Gena Showalter.

Offer valid from November 24, 2015, to December 31, 2015.
Redeemable at participating retail outlets. Not redeemable at Barnes & Noble.
Limit one coupon per purchase. Valid in the U.S.A. and Canada only.

52613047

Canadian Retailers: Harlequin Enterprises Limited will pay the face value of this coupon plus 10.25¢ if submitted by customer for this product only. Any other use constitutes fraud. Coupon is nonassignable. Void if taxed, prohibited or restricted by law. Consumer must pay any government taxes. Void if copied. Inmar Promotional Services ("IPS") customers submit coupons and proof of sales to Harlequin Enterprises Limited, P.O. Box 3000, Saint John, NB E2L 4L3, Canada. Non-IPS retailer—for reimbursement submit coupons and proof of sales directly to Harlequin Enterprises Limited, Retail Marketing Department, 225 Duncan Mill Rd., Don Mills, Ontario M3B 3K9, Canada.

5 65373 00076 2   (8100)0 12095

U.S. Retailers: Harlequin Enterprises Limited will pay the face value of this coupon plus 8¢ if submitted by customer for this product only. Any other use constitutes fraud. Coupon is nonassignable. Void if taxed, prohibited or restricted by law. Consumer must pay any government taxes. Void if copied. For reimbursement submit coupons and proof of sales directly to Harlequin Enterprises Limited, P.O. Box 880478, El Paso, TX 88588-0478, U.S.A. Cash value 1/100 cents.

® and ™ are trademarks owned and used by the trademark owner and/or its licensee.

© 2015 Harlequin Enterprises Limited

PHGS1215COUP

SPECIAL EXCERPT FROM

❤ HARLEQUIN®

Blaze

When Maddie Holmes first meets Mason Black she has no idea he's a Navy SEAL on an undercover mission… but she's about to find out all his secrets!

Read on for a sneak preview of
PLEASING HER SEAL by *Anne Marsh*
part of Harlequin Blaze's
UNIFORMLY HOT! miniseries.

Fantasy Island advertised itself as an idyllic slice of paradise located on the Caribbean Sea—the perfect place for a destination wedding or honeymoon. The elegant type on the resort brochure promised barefoot luxury, discreet hedonism and complete wish fulfillment. Maddie's job was to translate those naughty promises into sexy web copy that would drive traffic to her blog and fill her bank account with much-needed advertising dollars.

The summit beckoned, and she stepped out into a small clearing overlooking the ocean.

"Good view?" At the sound of the deep male voice behind her, Maddie flinched, arms and legs jerking in shock. Her camera flew forward as she scrambled backward.

Strong male fingers fastened around her wrist. Panicked, she grabbed her croissant and lobbed it at the guy, followed by her coffee. He cursed and dodged.

"It's not a good day to jump without a chute." He tugged her away from the edge of the lookout, and she got her first good look at him. Not a stranger. *Okay, then*.

HBEXP1215

Her heart banged hard against her rib cage, pummeling her lungs, before settling back into a more normal rhythm. *Mason*. Mason I-Can't-Be-Bothered-To-Tell-You-My-Last-Name-But-I'm-A-Stud. He led the cooking classes by the pool. She'd written him off as good-looking but aloof, not certain if she'd spotted a spark of potential interest in his dark eyes. Wishful thinking or dating potential—it was probably a moot point now, since she'd just pegged him with her mocha.

He didn't seem pissed off. On the contrary, he simply rocked back on his haunches, hands held out in front of him. *I come in peace*, she thought, fortunately too out of breath to giggle. The side of his shirt sported a dark stain from her coffee. Oh, goody. She'd actually scalded him. Way to make an impression on a poor, innocent guy. This was why her dating life sucked.

She tried to wheeze out an apology, but he shook his head.

"I scared you."

"You think?"

"That wasn't my intention." The look on his face was part chagrin, part repentance. Worked for her.

"I'll put a bell around your neck." Where had he learned to move so quietly?

"Why don't we start over?" He stuck out a hand. A big, masculine, slightly muddy hand. She probably shouldn't want to seize his fingers like a lifeline. "I'm Mason Black."

Don't miss PLEASING HER SEAL by Anne Marsh,
available January 2016 wherever
Harlequin® Blaze® books and ebooks are sold.

www.Harlequin.com

Copyright © 2016 by Anne Marsh

HBEXP1215

REQUEST YOUR FREE BOOKS!
2 FREE NOVELS PLUS 2 FREE GIFTS!

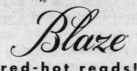

HARLEQUIN®

Blaze

red-hot reads!

YES! Please send me 2 FREE Harlequin® Blaze® novels and my 2 FREE gifts (gifts are worth about $10). After receiving them, if I don't wish to receive any more books, I can return the shipping statement marked "cancel." If I don't cancel, I will receive 4 brand-new novels every month and be billed just $4.74 per book in the U.S. or $5.21 per book in Canada. That's a savings of at least 14% off the cover price. It's quite a bargain. Shipping and handling is just 50¢ per book in the U.S. and 75¢ per book in Canada.* I understand that accepting the 2 free books and gifts places me under no obligation to buy anything. I can always return a shipment and cancel at any time. Even if I never buy another book, the two free books and gifts are mine to keep forever.

150/350 HDN GH2D

Name _____ (PLEASE PRINT) _____

Address _____ Apt. # _____

City _____ State/Prov. _____ Zip/Postal Code _____

Signature (if under 18, a parent or guardian must sign) _____

Mail to the **Reader Service:**
IN U.S.A.: P.O. Box 1867, Buffalo, NY 14240-1867
IN CANADA: P.O. Box 609, Fort Erie, Ontario L2A 5X3

Want to try two free books from another line?
Call 1-800-873-8635 or visit www.ReaderService.com.

* Terms and prices subject to change without notice. Prices do not include applicable taxes. Sales tax applicable in N.Y. Canadian residents will be charged applicable taxes. Offer not valid in Quebec. This offer is limited to one order per household. Not valid for current subscribers to Harlequin Blaze books. All orders subject to credit approval. Credit or debit balances in a customer's account(s) may be offset by any other outstanding balance owed by or to the customer. Please allow 4 to 6 weeks for delivery. Offer available while quantities last.

> **Your Privacy**—The Reader Service is committed to protecting your privacy. Our Privacy Policy is available online at www.ReaderService.com or upon request from the Reader Service.
>
> We make a portion of our mailing list available to reputable third parties that offer products we believe may interest you. If you prefer that we not exchange your name with third parties, or if you wish to clarify or modify your communication preferences, please visit us at www.ReaderService.com/consumerschoice or write to us at Reader Service Preference Service, P.O. Box 9062, Buffalo, NY 14240-9062. Include your complete name and address.

HBl5

Turn your love of reading into rewards you'll love with
Harlequin My Rewards

**Join for FREE today at
www.HarlequinMyRewards.com**

Earn **FREE BOOKS** of your choice.

Experience **EXCLUSIVE OFFERS** and contests.

Enjoy **BOOK RECOMMENDATIONS**
selected just for you.

PLUS! Sign up now
and get **500** points
right away!

Earn
FREE
REWARDS
Join
Today!
HarlequinMyRewards.com

MYR16R